The Cult

Trilogy (The Unofficial Minecraft Adventure Short Stories)

Mark Mulle

PUBLISHED BY:

Mark Mulle

Copyright © 2014

Disclaimer

This is a work of fiction. Names, characters, businesses, places, events and incidents are either the products of the author's imagination or used in fictitious manny. Any resemblance to actual persons, living or dead, or actual events is purely coincidental.

Author's Note: These short stories are for your reading pleasure. The characters in this "Minecraft Adventure Series" such as Steve, Endermen or Herobrine...etc are based on the Minecraft Game coming from Minecraft ®/TM & © 2009-2013 Mojang / Notch

Table of Contents

The Cult, Part One

Prologue

The light drizzle turned into a downpour, and Steve realized that he needed to find shelter—and fast. He was already about to catch a cold in this storm; the water seeped through the many gashes of his shirt, and no matter how he tried to avoid it, the rain managed to drench him. As he walked across this field, his movement stunted due to his injury, he heard a hissing sound behind him. When he turned around, he saw the familiar dead stare of the Creeper. Immediately, he unsheathed his sword, a crude steel blade that he had forged in a hurry. He began slashing at it with ferocity, screaming as he did. The Creeper fell down, disappearing in a puff of smoke. Creepers were commonplace, but this one caused his patience to fall apart. What was wrong with him?

The sun had set long ago, and he was surprised that he didn't run into any strong enemies, though he knew his luck was about to run out. If he didn't get out of here soon, he'd have to deal with mobs as well as the rain. There had to be somewhere where he could get some rest, although he didn't even know if he could sleep. He could fall face-first into a bed fit for a queen and would still have insomnia. Sighing, he saw a small forest to his left. He jumped inside, the trees providing a scarce amount of protection against the rain. Finally, he saw a tree that would give him shelter. It had a hole big enough for him to jump inside. There was hardly any space, but he would at least be out of the rain. His whole body screamed in pain, and he hoped that he could at least run slightly in the morning. Where he needed to go, he had to make it there as fast as possible. He peeked his head out of the hole on occasion so that he could see if he had been followed. However, there was no sign of anyone, so he concluded that he had lost him. The man would be onto him again soon, however, so all he could do was stay alert. However, he soon realized that doing this was more trouble than it was worth, as his eyelids objected to this idea. He soon closed them, and the lull of sleep embraced him. As he became conked out, his last thoughts were about Wendy.

Chapter One

"Nothing here, either? This is ticking me off!" Steve shouted as he slammed the book down. He felt himself seething, and normally, this would be a thing that only happened when someone pushed him one too many times. However, he grew angry after scouring every book in Glink's library, not being able to find a single one about the Ender Dragon. He sighed, and Wendy stood behind him as she tried to calm him down.

"I'm sorry," she said.

Steve ignored her apology. It had been almost a month since his brother transformed into the Ender Dragon, and he hadn't found any leads whatsoever. No one mentioned anything about a dragon flying overhead, no village had any books on the Ender Dragon, not even Chance's library. After failing to find a book on the Ender Dragon while visiting a few villages, they returned to Chance, only for their library to be vacant of books as well. The only thing that came close was a book on cryptids that briefly mentioned the Ender Dragon, but revealed that it was most likely a fictional story.

Steve tried to calm down. This was close to the twentieth town they had travelled to, and still there was no information on the Ender Dragon, and no one saw it flying. Sighing, Steve left the library, Wendy following him.

"Come on; let's go back to the inn," she proposed.

"Alright," Steve replied as they walked into the humble inn. They went to the second floor, unlocked the door, and stepped inside of the two-bed room. Steve immediately looked at Wendy, tears welling up in his eyes.

"I don't know what to do. I've been trying to stay strong, but with each passing day, it feels as though a weight is on my back. One that started off the size of a pebble but kept growing. I don't even know what to think anymore. Is my brother truly gone?"

Wendy hugged Steve, and he welcomed her arms. "Your brother is not gone. We can still save him, Steve. It's a big world, and we've just covered only a tiny dot of it. There has to be more information about the Ender Dragon."

Steve hoped so. The only thing he knew about the Ender Dragon was that it ruled from a dimension called The End, and three warriors slayed it, one of them keeping its blood until Steve's brother, Herobrine drank it. Steve tried to find out more information on The End as well but couldn't find anything at all.

As Steve calmed down, Wendy fell asleep on her bed. However, Steve could not. He took out his diamond sword and went outside, away from the village. He began swinging it, practicing all of his techniques. He soon ran into a tree and began to practice on that. Steve considered himself to be a competent swordsman, but the fact of the matter was that he failed to defeat his brother, so there always was room for improvement. Steve clashed his sword on the tree hard enough to slice it, and it came tumbling down. He began thinking about Herobrine. His brother was inside of that dragon, probably screaming for his life because he was trapped inside of a beast, one that had no desires except to destroy the world. The idea terrified him, and he swung his sword in anger. He began to pant as he tried to calm himself. He knew that he could not take on the Ender Dragon with all of the rage he had pent up, but it was so difficult. Blaming himself for Herobrine's transformation wore him down, especially when it technically was his fault. He dared him to drink the Ender Dragon's blood, and it didn't matter if he didn't know about what it was. Steve tried to forget about this fact and remember that there were other malevolent forces behind this, but he couldn't bring himself to forgive for the choices he had made. He sheathed his sword and decided to go back to the inn. Maybe a good night's rest would—

There was a group of people walking in the opposite direction of him, and they were all cloaked in black. Five in all, each marching in a trudging fashion, almost as if they were in deep thought. Steve wondered where they were heading to, and normally, he would just leave them be. However, one turned around to straighten their cloak.

The person didn't seem to notice Steve, but when Steve noticed the front of the cloak, his interest not only piqued a little from the sight of the purple eyes painted on the hood, but it skyrocketed also once he saw the jagged white cloth shaped like teeth on the edges of the hood, forming a mouth. Immediately, Steve thought of the Ender Dragon. Perhaps it was just a coincidence; for all he knew, these outfits could be an Enderman with teeth. He would have approached them and asked, but one glance at their front made him refrain. The person, from what little their hood revealed, had a pallid face as white as a skeleton, his lips as black as the Ender Dragon's blood itself. Steve decided to follow them instead. The possibility of a lead excited Steve, even though these cultish figures gave him a slight chill.

The field lacked any hiding places, but thankfully, the people did not turn around as Steve tailed them. He moved deftly, and soon the people began to ascend a steep hill. When they reached the peak, they started to go down, and when Steve reached the top, his jaw unhinged.

The hill circled an open valley. In the center, a bonfire roared, and a large ring of people surrounded the fire, chanting strange words that Steve could barely make out.

Ereo Zis Ender Ereo Zis Ender Ero.

They chanted these words in monotone as the members that Steve followed joined the circle. The chanting soon faded, and then one of the people in the circle stepped out and stood in front of the others. This one was in an outfit that was distinguishable from the others, specked in white, and his hood was pulled down. He had a pale face, slicked hair that was liquorish in color, and a pointed nose that almost looked sharp. His age was ambiguous; he could have been thirty, or he could have been sixty. His face gave off the exact amount of wrinkles where it could go either way.

"I see we have new believers who have submitted to the calling. Our numbers are increasing so fast, and soon the world will know the power of the Ender Dragon." The leader closed his eyes, a euphoric look on his face. "Can you all feel it? The power of the Ender Dragon is growing. It's still trying to adjust to its new vessel, lying dormant in

The End, but soon it will awaken, and this world will bow down to it! And we will be the ones who it will accept to be its servants!"

The other members cheered, sounding half-uninterested due to the monotone in their voice. The cult leader was the only one who had any personality to him, sounding cunning and regal. "Now then, for those who are new, I am Draven, and I am the descendant of the Claw of the Ender, Ryane. My ancestor fought valiantly to protect the dragon, but the chosen heroes slayed him. I shall avenge him and find the descendants of the heroes. And the Ender Dragon has given me hints as to where the heroes are. I can feel it! Some of them are around here. I can't tell how close or how far they are, but I can feel them. And once we kill them, the Ender Dragon will reign supreme with no challengers!"

Steve shuddered. So these guys were involved with the Ender Dragon. He didn't know what the Claw of the Ender was, and that excited him. He possibly could learn more about the Ender Dragon through them, but he did not want to go down there with his sword raised. He had taken on a group of thieves with no problem, but these people looked much more powerful, and soon his theory was proven correct.

"We'll meet up again two nights from now and discuss how we will find and handle these heroes. Until then, may the Ender Dragon's breath lead you to salvation."

As soon as he said this, Draven extended his right hand, and a powerful blast of wind blasted from his palm. It was strong enough to put out the fire as well as knock a few people back.

Is this a wizard? Steve thought, and he walked down the hill, getting away from these guys. He could just feel the power that came from Draven, power that made Herobrine look like a skeleton in comparison. Steve had to fall back and think of a plan.

When he went back to the inn, Wendy rested peacefully, and in her sleep, she looked so innocent. Steve almost felt a pang of guilt about having her come with him, even though she did it voluntarily. He supposed that they would plan their next move tomorrow, but for now, he needed some rest. His next enemy, while intimidating, would be defeated, even if he had to learn magic to do that. As he closed his eyes, he had trouble sleeping as the realization that this went deeper that he had even imagined dawned on him. But he would pull through it.

Chapter Two

As Steve woke up, Wendy was already dressed and bathed.

"You slept an hour late. It's a good thing I care and will allow you to get some sleep."

Steve rubbed his eyes, still feeling groggy. "Sorry, I couldn't sleep. So I trained and. . . Wait a minute; there's something I need to tell you."

Steve explained to Wendy about the cult that he'd encountered and how they were planning on finding the heroes who were destined to defeat the Ender Dragon. He also brought up Draven's powers.

"Well, it looks like we found our lead, but if he's as strong as you say he is, then we're in big trouble."

Steve nodded. "I'm wondering how in the world we're going to handle this. I've ran a few options through my head, and the only thing I can think of is that we should disguise ourselves. We need to create a robe that looks just like theirs. Powdering our skin would help too."

"Powdering our skin?"

Steve forgot that he didn't explain this to Wendy. "The cultists all had pale skin and blood red lips. None of them looked like they've been in the sun. It's eerie, to say the least."

"We should find everything we need in some of the stores around here. I'll let the innkeeper know that we'll be staying a few extra nights."

She went downstairs, and Steve wondered if this plan would even work. Did these people have a way of telling imposters from the true members, or did they assume that anyone who donned a cloak was one of them? Once Wendy went back to the room, she sighed.

"Hopefully, we can get more money soon. I'm milking my wallet for all that it's worth. Well, let's buy some cloaks, shall we?"

The two left the inn and stepped foot into the village. After his long stay in Chance, Glink was a breath of fresh air. It was a sizable village, much more expansive than his hometown, but small enough to navigate it. Steve and Wendy found the clothing store and went inside. Immediately, they were greeted by rows upon rows of clothes. Shirts, tunics, trousers, every type of clothing except for a hood. They went to the counter, and a thin middle-aged woman who had her graying hair tied back greeted them.

"What can I do for you two?" she asked.

Wendy spoke. "We're looking for a black cloak. Do you have any?"

She shook her head, a slight look of concern in her face. "I'm sorry, but it's not the season for those to be in stock."

Steve assumed that Wendy would give up, but instead she asked, "Do you have any black, white, and purple fabric, as well as materials to sew with?"

"That I do," the lady replied as she entered the room behind them. Meanwhile, Wendy grabbed two black tunics from the shelves as they waited, and when she returned, Wendy paid for everything. Once the two left, Steve looked behind him, wondering why the shopkeeper seemed a tad worried.

They arrived back at the inn, and Wendy spoke. "Yes, I can sew to save my life. My father's side of the family created the weapons shop in Chance, but my mother's side ran a clothing business. Her business was pulled under shortly after she married my father, but she taught me how to sew and how to create my own style of clothing. I haven't done it in a while, but it's like anything in that it comes back to you once you do it again."

Steve watched Wendy as she began to work her magic, and Steve instructed her on what the hoods looked like, telling her to cut a hole there and to sew there. Wendy soon knew what she was doing, however, and began sewing frantically, much to Steve's surprise. This woman was full of surprises. She sewed the black fabric onto the tunic to create a hood and then sewed some fabric on the bottom to make it longer. She cut out two holes on top of the hood and sewed the purple fabric to create eyes, meticulously cutting the purple fabric into two circles. Then she cut the white fabric into evenly-sized triangles and sewed them around the hood. In no time at all, she had created two hoodies that resembled the cultists' hoods to a T.

"It's a little crude, but I think it'll work," she told Steve.

"Crude? This looks great! You're a natural," Steve replied, and Wendy warmly smiled at him. He tried the larger black hood on. It fit him perfectly—tight enough to securely stay around him but loose enough to give him that "ominous cultist" feel. Wendy tried her outfit on as well, admiring how it fit over her too.

"Now what?" Steve asked.

"We'll save the makeup for tomorrow. Right now, we should just have fun. It'll be two nights from now, so let's just relax."

Steve agreed, and the two walked around the village. Despite Steve trying to have fun, he had a difficult time doing so. They tried to fish at a pond outside of the village, renting some fishing supplies from a local store, but Steve couldn't find the drive to fish. He easily could find it back when he had fished with Jonish, which was immediately after the showdown with Herobrine, but he assumed that the weight of what had happened had not hit him at that point. Steve smiled as he cast his rod, but inside he didn't feel like catching anything. When his lure sunk, he lightly tugged, not giving the pole enough power for the hook to secure the fish. Meanwhile, Wendy caught a medium-sized birdfish, claiming that this was the first time in ages that she had actually fished.

The next day, the two went to a beauty store, which was located next to the clothing shop. Once they entered, the aroma of various perfumes permeated the air. Even Wendy coughed slightly. The woman at the counter, a regal-looking lady covered in diamonds and coated in makeup, asked what they needed. Wendy requested the best powder and lipstick that they had, and she reached under the counter and pulled out a case of powder and a tube of lipstick.

"The powder is made from Creeper ash, and the lipstick is made from redstone. It's the finest stuff around here."

Wendy paid for it, and the two left. They once again tried to have fun, but Steve couldn't bring himself to do it. Meanwhile, they kept noticing signs popping up. They were located outside of stores, at the fountain in the square, and all around. Each advertised one thing.

"HARVEST DANCE TONIGHT!"

An old lady stood in front of one of them, and she turned around to face the two. "I can tell that you two are outsiders. The Harvest Dance is what you think it is. A dance for a good harvest and for having fun. You should go to it; I met my first love at the harvest dance sixty years ago!" she began to chortle as he left, and the two looked at each other.

"Why not?" Wendy asked. Steve nodded as well. As they continued on, they found a shop set up close to the square, saying that customers could rent dresses and suits for cheap. The man running the stand, a classy-looking mustachioed fellow, only had two articles of clothing left, a red dress and a suit. Steve paid for the outfits this time, and the two went back to the inn, waiting for the sun to set.

When it became dark, Wendy went to the restroom to dress while Steve put on his outfit. He went from a shaggy-haired boy who wore a tattered green shirt to someone who looked much classier. His black dress pants complemented his dark suit, and it even came with a bow tie that he finally managed to put on. He looked quite dapper, and he looked even more so after he combed his hair a bit. As he did that, Wendy walked out. When Steve saw her, his cheeks reddened slightly.

Steve thought that Wendy was pretty but didn't see her as someone who blew him away. However, this Wendy looked absolutely stunning. She tied her long red hair back, cleaning it until it radiated like the sun. The dress on her fit perfectly and blended in with said hair, and it contrasted well with her light skin. She had used some of the makeup, applying a dab of white powder on her face and a bit of lipstick on her lips.

"You look great," Steve replied, knowing that his compliment was a complete understatement.

She smiled. "Thanks. You don't look bad yourself. Now then, let's do some dancing."

At the town square, the festivities had already begun. A small group of traveling musicians played their drums, ukuleles, and pipes joyously, bringing out the dance in everyone. Merchants saw this as an ample time to sell their best wares, and the scammers were out on the prowl. Steve was stopped at least twice by two merchants who claimed to have a cure-all potion made from swamp grass that could make him live to be two-hundred. Steve refused, and the two went to the center.

As they did, the music changed from festive to a slow ballad, and Wendy extended her hand to Steve. "Come on; let's dance," she encouraged, and Steve grabbed her hand. He did not have a clue what he was doing, and seeing the other dancers broke his confidence. The others waltzed with their partners perfectly, while Steve awkwardly spun Wendy around, failing to grab her hand. Wendy was a little better with the slow dancing, but her movements were slightly stiff as well. However, she was smiling.

"It's not a competition; it's just a night to have fun!" she told him. Steve smiled, feeling slightly embarrassed, but he knew that she had a point. He tried to ignore the people around them and make it their night to have fun. He hadn't had a night where he could be himself in so long, and this was a refreshing break from that. As Steve danced with Wendy, he could feel his troubles melting away. For one night, he could forget about the stresses that faced him and the dread of having to disguise themselves to infiltrate the cult.

When the music stopped and the dancers began to go home, Steve and Wendy were still dancing until the two were aware that the dance had ended. The two went back to the inn and began to formulate their plan for tomorrow night.

"We should bring our weapons in case things go sour," Wendy suggested. Steve agreed, but added something to that.

"I'm a little worried. We have the strongest weapons, but this guy has power. He could blow them away with just a wave of his hand. I'd prefer for us to be careful and not have to worry about that."

Wendy agreed, and the two fell asleep shortly after. When they woke up, they spent their hours biding their time, knowing that it would be later in the night until the cult would meet again. An hour before their assumed time, they began to put on the outfit. Steve watched as Wendy coated her face with excessive powder and painted her lips until they were as red as blood. Once she put the hood on, she went to Steve, carrying the makeup in her hand.

"Oh, dear," Steve said as she powdered him down, with Steve trying to suppress a sneeze. Once that was taken care of, she covered his lips with lipstick, and then when that was done, he put up his hood. The two looked in the mirror, and both looked identical and genderless. Steve could barely breathe under the excessive makeup, and he couldn't wait until this was all over.

Chapter Three

The two left the inn and walked across the village, being thankful that no one spotted them. As they left the outskirts, they saw another member walking from the village. Without thinking, the two huddled close to the person, who did not turn around. Eventually, more members came from other directions and melded into the group, and soon they had a crew. Steve and Wendy tried to walk in a cultish fashion, hoping that they blended in perfectly. Steve's heart pounded like a drum, and he hoped that no one noticed.

Finally, it was time to climb the hill. The two walked up it, trying not to pant, and then they reached the apex and saw the raging fire below. They made it to the circle of other members and joined in, and Draven removed his hood once again.

"Ahh, I see that this group is getting larger by the day. Welcome new members, and may the Ender Dragon breathe its breath upon you. To sum up what was said in last night's meaning, I promised that I would give details on how we are going to handle the heroes who are destined to slay the Ender Dragon. I can feel it; a few of the heroes are close by. In this meeting, I'll elaborate on how to handle them."

Draven cleared his throat, and spoke two words. "Kill them."

The crowd cheered, and Steve and Wendy gave their own monotone praises as well. Once it died down, Draven elaborated more. "The problem with our ancestors and why they failed was that they were too soft. They were trying to slow down the heroes, and they would hold back when they fought them or gloat too long. There will be none of that, brothers and sisters. Once we see the heroes, we will aim to kill. No words, no giving them a chance. This way, there will be no one to stop the Ender Dragon, who will reign supreme on the land."

The crowd cheered again, and Steve's heart fluttered. These guys were not dancing around. Even Herobrine gave Steve multiple chances. In the sewers, he could have simply stabbed Steve and gotten it over with, but instead he threw Steve into the waterfall below and hoped that he would survive. Attacking them head-on would be a dumb idea, so the two blended in for a while now.

"Now then, you may be wondering how we are going to find them. Well, I received a huge lead from one of our members. She runs the clothing store in Glink, proving that we are ordinary people who blend in with society."

Oh no oh no oh no oh no oh no, Steve's mind raced. Wendy sweated as well, her makeup running a bit. The two didn't need Draven to continue to realize what had happened. The middle-aged woman who ran the clothing store was a member of the cult, and there was no wonder why she seemed concerned when Steve and Wendy wanted to purchase clothes from her.

"According to her, a man and a woman came in asking for hoodies, and when she said that she had none, the woman asked for fabric that was the same colors as our hoods. That may be a coincidence, but I believe that there are no coincidences. There heroes know about us, and for all we know, they could be in this group right now!"

The cult members began chattering, and Steve and Wendy acted frantic as well. The members were accusing one another of being an imposter, their evidence ranging from the length of their hood to how they walked.

"Silence!" Draven shouted and everyone calmed down. "It's just a hunch, like I said, and we don't need to go off on one another just yet. Relanda, come here!"

One of the members walked beside Draven, and when they took off their hood, it was revealed that Relanda was the name of the clothing store shopkeep. She looked unrecognizable in all of that makeup and looked uglier with it on.

"It's simple, really. All we have to do is have everyone remove their hoods, and Relanda will see if anyone remotely resembles the two who purchased the clothes. It's a common sense solution, and immediately when she sees the two, we'll destroy them. No questions. I don't care if they just resemble the two of them, we should always play it—"

While the group was fixated, Steve and Wendy immediately ran away from the circle, taking off their hoods to increase their movements. Draven was dumbfounded for a few seconds, but he began to laugh. "That was easy. Now die!"

Draven extended his hand, and as Steve looked back, a few fireballs flew toward the hill. Steve and Wendy jumped out of the way and got away from the radius of the explosion as they made it to the top. That was when Draven, from all the way down there, fired a blast of wind from his hand. Immediately, Steve and Wendy were knocked back and began rolling down the hill. Once they reached the foot, the two writhed in pain but stood up and began running again as the cult made it to the peak. However, the two were already far away from the cult, and their feet moved so fast that they were away by the time they made it back to the village. The two ran to the inn and went back to their rooms, and immediately, they began to pack their supplies. Their food, their canteens, their pickaxes—everything needed to be packed.

"We have to get as far away from here as poss—"

"Steve, look!"

Steve stared through the window that Wendy pointed out of, and he noticed that a large portion of the village was in flames. Walking down the dirt road was Draven, and his finger pointed at buildings, a blast of fire coming from the tip. Immediately, the building became scorched. People ran from him and abandoned the village. Steve slipped on his diamond armor, and then Steve and Wendy went downstairs, passing the confused innkeeper, hearing Draven shout.

"Heroes, come out to play! I'll burn this village down if you don't, because I know you're still here!"

"We need to run!" Wendy shouted

"No, we need to stop this village from being attacked. People will lose their homes and possibly their own lives because of this. I have a lot of things on my conscious right now, and I don't want it to grow even more."

Before Wendy could say anything, Steve stood in front of Draven, waving his arms as he did. "Over here!" he taunted.

"Hmph, bad move, kid!"

Draven immediately blasted fire at Steve, but Steve turned around, letting his diamond armor absorb the blaze as he ran off. The diamond armor did not heat up when worn, unlike steel, and he only felt a few degrees hotter. He grabbed Wendy, and the two ran, close enough to see Draven as he followed him but far enough so that they could avoid his attacks. They soon ran from the village, and Draven left the scorching place behind. From what Steve saw, there were no casualties, but he knew that many people would lose their homes and their precious memories because of this. Once they were in the field, this area gave some variety. There were plateaus, dips, and animals roaming around, giving the two enough room to strategize. Steve felt like an animal himself, a defenseless deer chased by a hunter.

Draven cackled as the fields were set ablaze, his eyes almost as red as the violent flames that surrounded him.

"Face me, cowards! Unless you want this land to become scorched as well!"

Steve ignored his cries and continued to run, and soon the field changed from grassy to a tad rocky, and the two ran into a cliff. The drop wasn't too far, but it would hurt if they fell. There was a rickety bridge that extended to the other side, and Steve wondered if they could make it without the two of them falling.

Steve suddenly had an idea. One of them needed to get there safely, and another needed to fend off Draven. There was only one person who could do that.

As Draven closed in on them, Steve said to Wendy "Cross the bridge! I'll hold him back and give you enough time to cross. If we go together, he'll probably destroy the bridge."

The objection came. "But Steve, you need to come with me! I can't be alone!" Wendy shouted, and Steve's heart sank.

"Don't worry; I'll follow when I fend him off. I'm not going to lose you a second time," Steve promised, even though he wasn't sure.

Wendy wanted to object some more, but instead she nodded. "Alright, but don't die on me."

Wendy ran across the bridge while Steve sprinted toward Draven, getting his attention. Already, he bought enough time for Wendy to cross.

"Well, that was clever. But it was all for nothing. We will find her, and then we shall kill her. Just like we're about to do to you," Draven promised.

"I don't think so!" Steve shouted, and he swung his sword. Draven held his hand up, looking as though he were about to catch the blade. All of a sudden, his arm changed into diamond, looking as though he had grafted the arm of a beautiful diamond statue to him.

Once his sword hit the arm, the diamond sword shattered, fragments flying everywhere. "Oops. I forgot to mention that not only have I mastered the magic elements, but I can also change my body into any mineral that I want. Silly me."

Steve hopped back, his jaw unhinged, and then Draven extended his arm again, trying to blow him back. His diamond armor, however, withstood the blow, and Steve was only pushed a few inches. Draven then tried to burn Steve, but his armor seemed to absorb the blow as he turned around.

"Hmm, that diamond armor is a bit of a nuisance, isn't it? Well, I suppose I should rectify that."

Draven's hand changed to diamond again, and that's when he charged toward Steve, raising his fist up. Steve tried to run, but Draven's fist punched into his back. His back erupted in pain and would have shattered if the diamond armor didn't absorb most of the blow. His armor began to crack, and soon it crumbled from him. Draven ran toward him again and swiped his helmet, and then his legs became diamond. He jumped up, and his feet hit the tip of Steve's diamond boots. When he jumped off, Steve's feet erupted in pain, and his boots shattered. Immediately, Steve began to run toward the bridge, feeling the rickety planks below him.

"Dumb move!" Draven shouted, and that's when his finger shot a flamethrower of fire, bathing over the ropes that supported the bridge. Immediately, Steve could feel the bridge sinking as the ropes thinned. If he could make it to the end, he would—

Snap!

The bridge fell, and Steve dropped down with it. When the bridge smashed on the rock below, Steve braced for impact. Once it slammed onto the ground, intense pain screamed in both legs. Nothing felt broken, but as he walked from the bridge's ruins, he discovered that he couldn't go fast without pain erupting. His legs were most likely an angel hair's length from shattering.

He was in pain, but he knew that he would be in so much more if he didn't get out of here. Above him, Draven watched, shooting fireballs at him. Steve noticed a hole in the ground straight ahead, and he fell inside just as the fireballs rained down above. He slid down a tunnel, and when the explosions happened, the hole above him was sealed up, rubble collapsing around him.

He crawled deeper into a tunnel, finding a tipped chunk of steel pointing from the rock to the right of him. He grabbed it. Eventually, the tunnel opened up, and he popped out from the side of a rocky wall, another lush field in front of him. There were a few twigs below him, and Steve fastened the steel to the twig, creating the most awful-looking sword imaginable. As he looked above him, he noticed that the clouds were becoming dark.

An hour later, he hid from the storm inside of a tree.

Chapter Four

The fear of the unknown was something that frightened humans the most. The fear of death, the fear of what was to come tomorrow and the fear of how people would think about you surrounds people's minds every day. The fear of the unknown was particularly hitting Wendy as she ran as fast as her legs could take her. She listened to Steve when he told her to run, and she did not look back no matter how much she had the urge to. She knew that Steve was a great fighter and lucky when it came to survival, but this was an entirely different game altogether. Draven had power that she could not even fathom, and she knew that Steve would have a challenge in fighting him. She almost wanted to go back, but she knew that she had to run.

The unknown clouded her. Steve could be alive and well, standing above Draven as he begged for mercy. He could have escaped or could have gotten away with a fatal injury. Or Draven could have kidnapped him, but she doubted that. Draven stated that he would kill first, ask questions later, and she doubted that he would throw Steve into a river and just hope that he drowned. He would most likely skewer Steve and then throw him into a volcano, making sure that he was dead.

After her feet could not run any more, she finally turned around. No sign of Draven anywhere. She wanted to go back, but she knew that she had to keep running. If Draven saw her, she was as good as dead. All she carried right now was a diamond sword. In normal cases, this would suffice, but she felt like she needed ten tons of TNT just to feel safe. Sighing, she saw that the clouds were letting out a light drizzle, and she could not see any sign of a shelter just yet. She wondered if the village was okay, and she hoped the rain would put out the fires. She also missed Steve a whole lot. Normally, this would just mean that she missed his company, but she could feel something more. Feelings for him, in particular. She enjoyed dancing with him and wished to do it again, and she felt so alone right now. After resting, she continued to run, and that's when she saw a horse-drawn carriage galloping down a dirt road, the driver inside of the carriage. When it saw Wendy, the horse slowed down, eventually coming to a stop.

The doors of the carriage opened, and an aristocratic woman with honey-blonde hair gave her a signal to come in. Wendy was skeptical at first, but then the downpour happened. Immediately, she ran into the carriage and shut the door.

Inside of the carriage, the driver, a mustachioed man in a suit, controlled the horses by holding reins connected to the outside. Meanwhile, the woman spoke to Wendy.

"Are you okay? It looked like you were running away from something."

Wendy started panting. "Yeah, a wizard is out to kill me."

The woman let out a laugh that was as rich as her bank account, and Wendy knew there was no use. "Not really. I was just running away from the storm."

The woman nodded. "Ahh. I'm Lady Elena, and I'm returning to my mansion. I can let you stay there until the storm dies down, if that's okay with you."

"Yes, please," Wendy replied, wondering if her mansion would be at risk. She had outrun Draven, but for how long? The man controlling the horses whipped the reins and made them gallop faster, and Wendy looked outside of the window at the surrounding fields. No sign of Draven here. She guessed that she really had outrun him. She just wondered if Steve had as well.

"So, tell me more about yourself," Lady Elena asked.

"Oh. I'm a weapons seller from Chance," Wendy replied.

"Oooh, Chance. I heard you could get richer than a king in that town, but I never trusted it. Instead, I became a miner and struck it big one day, finding more diamonds than you could count. Who said that hard work doesn't pay off?"

Wendy chuckled. "I'll turn those diamonds into weapons, if you'd like," she told her.

Lady Elena chuckled. "I'm a pacifist, dearie. And besides, I sold them a long time ago."

They made some more small talk, with Wendy eventually looking out of the window again. The road ahead turned to gravel and then paved stone, and soon the mansion in front of her loomed closer. It was three stories tall with a huge garden, and she couldn't even imagine the back of it. The carriage stopped in front of the iron gate, and the man driving the carriage hopped out and opened it. Then the carriage went through, and the man got out again to close it. The fence should have made Wendy safe, but she knew that Draven could easily blow it to bits if she needed to. The carriage went toward the entrance, and the man got out again, coming back with an umbrella. He handed it to Lady Elena, and she stepped out, Wendy waddling close to her to avoid the rain. Eventually, they made it to the front door, and Wendy walked inside. She was safe for now, but she hoped that Steve had survived. The idea of him dying frightened her, and she almost had an anxiety attack, thinking about such a thing.

When Steve woke up, the storm had ended, and Steve climbed out of the tree. His legs were still in pain, but they felt slightly better, which was an improvement to say the least. Maybe they would heal up later today. He wondered where he should go, and then it hit him. Wendy was gone, and Steve didn't know where she had gone or if she was even still alive. For all he knew, she could have been killed by Draven. While he burned down the bridge, and while there didn't appear to be any close place to cross, he wondered if Draven could cross easily. If he could turn his entire body into diamond, then maybe he could simply jump over or turn into a spider and climb up to the other side. His stomach ached as he thought of Wendy's fate. She was such a sweet girl, and she'd already had enough bad stuff happen to her, including her being slaved to work for Herobrine. Sighing, Steve took out his poor excuse for a sword and walked deeper into the woods. He didn't know where this would take him, but staying in the woods would be a good idea, considering there were plenty of places to hide in case Draven found them again. He also wondered where Draven had gone. It had been hours upon hours since he had escaped from Draven, and he assumed that Draven had either lost him or thought that he had killed Steve. If it was the latter case, then Wendy was in even more danger than Steve once believed. Draven had said that he would kill both of them, after all.

He began to think about his position as a hero as well. Did Draven believe that he was the descendant of the three heroes who slayed the Ender Dragon? Because Steve did not feel like a hero currently. If anything, he felt like a loser, one who could not even defeat the Ender Dragon's main follower. Sighing, he walked deeper into the woods. A skeleton approached him and fired an arrow, but Steve blocked it with his sword and carried on. Confused, the skeleton rattle away, not knowing what to think about Steve.

Eventually, the forest cleared up, and Steve walked down a field again. His mind kept fixating on Wendy. Not only did he miss her company, but he also missed everything about her. The way she always encouraged him even when he was down, the way she always had pep to her, the way she danced—it all seem to permeate his mind. Was he going mad? He had no interest in girls before this; quite frankly, the idea of dating was something that he didn't want to try until he was at least thirty. His emotions were jumbled right now, and he felt like they would be until he found Wendy again.

He drew a sigh as he saw something looming ahead of him. It towered above, and seemed to grow larger as he hopped on the road. It wasn't as expansive as a castle, but it was definitely a mansion, to say the least. Other than the mansion, there didn't appear to be any other form of civilization, and Steve wondered if it was even safe to go in there. An iron gate blocked his way into it, but on the side of the gate, he noticed a button. He pressed it down and heard a voice coming from an intercom above the button.

"Who is it?" a woman asked.

"I'm Steve. I'm looking for some—"

"Steve! Let him in! He's my friend!" another voice clamored. It belonged to one person only, and that was Wendy.

"Wendy!" Steve shouted, joy returning to his tired voice.

"I shall let Jerkin open the gate," the lady replied.

The doors of the mansion opened, and a fanciful butler walked out. He removed a key from the pocket of his coat and unlocked the gate, pulling it open. Steve went on through and greeted who he assumed was Jerkin. Deep down, he was thankful that the two of them were not separated for longer.

"What should we do about the two of them?" one of the cult members asked on the following night. The person under the hood felt brave asking that, since Draven appeared to be irritable ever since the meeting.

"We have to find them," Draven stated. "This time, we'll all strike. I thought I could take them on by myself, but they managed to slip away. I thought that I had buried the boy, but I can still feel his presence. He is alive and well, but before too long, he won't be. I have plans in store for him."

Draven tried to sound cocky, but in reality, this whole crisis troubled him. He had never had so much trouble in dealing with just two people. While it was true that he outmatched the boy, that kid was clever, managing to slip away like a magician. His first flaw was not bringing his other members. After the incident, he dismissed them eventually, saying that he would handle it on his own. He was embarrassed at the fact that someone knew about his meetings, someone he assumed was the hero who would defeat the Ender Dragon again.

"Where could they be though?" one asked.

Draven rubbed his chin, thinking of the possibilities. Then he realized something. "Aha. I might know where they are."

"Do tell!"

"I don't know where that hole leads, but there is a mansion close to where the girl escaped. A storm happened shortly after I lost them as well. Unless the owner is a cruel, heartless person, the girl probably ran into the mansion, seeking shelter there. Tomorrow, we shall see. We won't assault the mansion unless they are in there and won't come out."

The crowd gave their cheers as everyone was dismissed. Draven put out the fire, and then when everyone was gone, he disappeared. When he reappeared, he stood in a room that should not have existed. There was no structure, no light, and it didn't provide any ways to exist. Even more of a paradox was the fact that he could see himself fine, as well as the creature in the center.

The creature was entirely black and should have blended in with the room entirely, but Draven could distinguish it from the rest of the void. The creature appeared to be sleeping, but Draven knew that it could hear him even if he whispered. Even when in the recovery stage, the Ender Dragon could see and hear all.

"I'm sorry that I've yet to kill them, Master. But don't worry. I think I've figured out where they are, and they're in for a rude awakening once I assault them," Draven stated. Usually, his voice was filled with confidence, but in front of the Ender Dragon, it sounded meek, almost as though it begged for mercy. The Ender Dragon did not respond, but Draven knew that it heard him. It currently rested in a pocket dimension that branched from The End. Here, it rested, absorbing the darkness that surrounded it. While the Ender Dragon was powerful enough already, it still needed lots of rest before it reawakened as the ruler of this world. Inside of it, it still had the soul of the boy who consumed the dragon's blood, and it needed to gain its powers back. Draven saw it as someone who had broken their legs and would take months to recover, gradually gaining back their strength, taking baby steps. The Ender Dragon was doing the same thing, and when it awakened, it would have all of its power, and the boy who existed inside of it would finally be extinguished, consumed by the Ender Dragon's black soul. The idea made Draven giddy; his ancestors had worked hard in order for this plan to work, and his grandmother was the one who delivered the black blood to the boy. This plan was coming into fruition like clockwork, and when it was over, they would all pay for their crimes against the world.

Chuckling, Draven teleported out, removing his hood as he went back to the Overworld. The sun would be rising soon, and the castle would be calling him to do his work. He let his hair down, revealing that his slicked-back hair was shoulder-length, and his skin began to change from pale to creamy. Finally, he allowed himself to teleport, ending up in the watchtower of a castle. Thankfully, he would just cast a few spells, and that would be it; then he could bring his wrath down upon the heroes and the person who kept them in the mansion if he needed to.

Chapter Five

Their reunion was a sweet one. When Steve saw Wendy sitting on the expansive table in the dining room, Steve forgot all about his pain and ran toward Wendy, embracing her with a hug. Meanwhile, Wendy did the same. The lady and the butler let the two be for their reunion, leaving the room altogether.

"I thought you were dead," Wendy told him.

"Nah, it will take more than that to kill me," Steve replied.

"How did you survive?" she asked.

"I don't know myself. This man is more powerful than even my brother. He can change himself to diamond after all, and he used that to shatter my weapons and armor."

Wendy gasped. Then Steve explained how he fell down with the bridge but managed to escape through a hole just as Draven sent a flurry of fireballs his way. Wendy felt upset as Steve described him having to stay inside of a tree for the night, feeling guilty that she slept in a bed that was heaven in a mattress, even though she still struggled to fall asleep.

"Are you going to be okay? Your legs are in pain, after all."

Steve wondered that himself. He needed to get better if he wanted to fight or, rather, *evade* Draven.

"Here, I'll get Lady Elena," Wendy said as she left the dining room. When she returned with Elena, the lady looked legitimately concerned for Steve.

"Don't worry; I'll prepare you a salt bath. It relieves the pain and fixes you up in less than an hour."

"Thanks for all that you've done," Steve said. For someone wealthy, she was courteous. He hoped that they wouldn't put her in danger of Draven's wrath, however. She did not deserve that. All Draven had to do was punch the gate with his diamond hand, and it would break it like a bundle of sticks. He just hoped that Draven had no clue where they were.

When it was prepared, Elena took Steve to the bathing room, an expansive area where the bath was the size of a miniature pool, the water steaming hot, a dish of fresh fruit on its side. Elena closed the door, and Steve took off his clothes, limping toward the bath. The repercussions from him running toward Elena were hitting him hard, and all he wanted to do was relax for a little while.

His toes dipped in the hot water, and it felt a little scalding for his tastes. However, he knew that the rules for cold water also applied to piping hot water as well. He just dealt with it and plopped his whole body in there. As soon as he sunk into the water, his skin soon adjusted, and he loved its warmth. His legs began to loosen, and the pain slowly evaporated; his negative emotions soon followed. He felt tranquil, which he hadn't been for quite some time. His anger seemed to fade as well, so he could actually fight with strategy the next time. He was just glad that he had gone off on a Creeper instead of something that could use his anger to their advantage, taking him out by creating a trap.

Thirty minutes passed, and his legs felt like new again. All he needed to do was just relax for a little while longer and then—

There was a loud knock on the door. "Steve, we have a big problem!" Wendy shouted from behind.

Immediately, Steve hopped out of the bath. His legs still ached, as he hadn't stayed in there long enough, but they felt much better than before.

Steve wrapped a towel around him and opened the door. "What is it?" he asked.

"Someone's at the gates, asking for us. I believe it's Draven. I told Elena to hold him off as soon as possible, but he probably isn't a very patient pers—"

Suddenly, the two heard an explosion from the outside. From what Steve saw, it came from the window in the bathroom, which he had paid no mind to before. Steve closed the door, slipped on his clothes, and observed from the window, which faced the entrance of the mansion. The gate was blown back, smoldering, its figure twisted and melted in some places. A group of hooded people marched past the gate's ruins, all being led by what appeared to be Draven.

No, already? I don't even have any weapons or armor. I'll be creamed! And this woman's mansion will be destroyed because of what we did!

Steve ran out, and then Wendy joined him. Steve didn't even bother to grab his crude sword; it would be like trying to kill a giant using a toothpick. It just wasn't going to happen. As they went down the corridor, Lady Elena and Jerkin joined them.

"Who are these people? I tried to say that I might have people like that, but they left, and then he blew the gate down with just his finger!"

"I wasn't joking when I said that a wizard was trying to kill us," Wendy said.

"I see that," Lady Elena replied. "But how are we going to repel them? I don't carry any weapons with me."

"We just have to escape," Steve said. "But how are we going to do that?"

"I built an escape tunnel in case something like this was going to happen, but I need to grab my fortune as well. It's sealed in a vault at the—"

Another explosion occurred. Steve and Wendy looked down the corridor and to the main room. The cult used their magic to burn the room down and make objects burst into pieces.

"There's no time!" Jerkin said. "Lady, we need to get out of here."

"I know I can get more diamonds, but this mansion—I spent years building this place, getting it just right, and now it's going to be burnt down, and it's because I let you two in!" Her calm demeanor shattered, she suddenly looked like a monster. The once pretty woman had a slew of wrinkles and veins popping from her face.

"It's not their fault, Lady," Jerkin said. "Let's just make our escape and then get out of here."

Trying to keep her composure, Elena said, "Right," and ran down the corridor. She opened a door and ran inside, and the three followed her. Her own room was decorated in jewels and gold, with a bookshelf the size of a library at the end of it.

"It should be this one," Lady Elena muttered to herself, pulling out a black book. At once, the bookshelf began to turn slowly, revealing a passageway as it moved to its side.

"I never thought I'd use this. This will take us to a tunnel that will lead us to an island. My father lives there. He's a wizard himself."

"A wizard?" Steve asked.

"Well, he's an alchemist and can enchant weapons," Elena replied. She looked at Wendy. "I kind of lied when I said that I found the diamonds. He has the power to turn rocks into diamonds, and he knew that I wanted to live like a celebrity, so he let me have it in the exchange that I use it for good. I'm sorry that I got mad. You two can explain to me what happened after we escape."

They ran through the passage as the bookshelf closed. While they did that, Steve's mind began racing.

An enchanting wizard? Steve wondered a few things about this. If he could easily create diamond weapons for them and then enchant them, would it be enough for them to defeat Draven with? The idea could work, but he would find out soon enough. Right now, they needed to get out of here. The passageway eventually stopped, leading to an open hole with a ladder going down. Steve noticed a switch on the wall to the right of the hole that Elena pressed.

"What's that do?" Wendy asked.

"This mansion has enough TNT behind its walls to turn this place into a giant candle. This switch will activate it and give us five minutes to escape. They're going to burn up my mansion regardless, so I want them to go along with it. Don't worry, once we reach the bottom, we won't be harmed."

Frantically, they climbed down the ladder, which went down for what seemed like hours. When the four reached the bottom, a rocky passageway lit by a few torches, they heard a rumbling sound above them. A few pebbles fell from the ceiling, but nothing happened other than that.

"I think that should deal with your wizard problem. Not even the strongest can survive that explosion."

I wouldn't be so sure about that, Steve thought. While it was wishful thinking that it had killed Draven, he doubted an explosion even at that magnitude would even hurt him. As they went down the passage, he hoped that this wizard would be able to help them out. Steve and Wendy looked at each other, and both of them sighed, feeling like two rats trying to escape from a giant cat. This chase game needed to end.

The Cult, Part Two

Chapter One

The water dripped from the ceiling, pattering on Steve's head as they went down the passage. Lady Elena kept explaining that this tunnel was at the bottom of the sea, so naturally there would be leakage. Wendy looked up, wondering if the tunnel would burst open and sweep them away. However, Lady Elena assured them that this tunnel would last years.

The path went on for quite a while. Elena claimed that she hadn't used it since she built the tunnel, instead relying on her fancy ship to get to her island where her father was. Steve needed to meet her father, as Elena claimed that he had the power to enchant weapons, something Steve needed to do in order to defeat Draven, the cult leader who was chasing after them. Elena didn't worry about him, saying that he perished when she activated the self-destruct mechanism inside of her house, but Steve doubted that. Draven was a powerful sorcerer, and it made Steve fear the idea of facing the Ender Dragon when the time was right. Even though his brother was trapped inside, he'd have to not hold back if he wanted to win.

"How much longer?" Steve asked, his knees aching. He still was in pain after the events of yesterday, even though the bath in Lady Elena's tub rejuvenated him for the most part.

"Just a little more. My father doesn't live too far out," Lady Elena replied.

"It feels like we've been walking miles," Wendy complained.

"Don't complain about the lady's tunnel," her butler, Jerkin, replied.

"There we go!" Lady Elena shouted, and Steve saw the end of the tunnel, which was a giant ladder leading upwards. Elena hopped on first, and Steve and Wendy followed. The climb up was quite a chore, and at times the ladder felt wobbly. However, they made it to the top without too much of a hassle, and as they reached it, they were in a small room made of stone. A door was ahead of them, and they stepped outside.

The four stood on a beach, their shoes sinking into the sand. They walked out of a small building that stood on this beach, and when they looked ahead at the waters, they couldn't see the other side where Lady Elena's mansion stood, or in this case, once stood.

"I haven't been to the beach in so long," Wendy claimed. "If it weren't for the fact that we're being chased and we have to save the world, I'd say that we should go for a swim."

Now that Steve thought about it, he hadn't been to a beach in his life. Immediately, his mind recalled him as a child looking at a picture book.

"That's supposed to be a desert," he told Herobrine.

"I don't think I want to go there. It sounds way too hot," Herobrine replied.

Steve flipped to the next page, an illustration of a beach, complete with a happy sun. "What about the beach?" he asked.

"Ooh, I'd love to go there. I've heard so many good things."

At that time, it was just pretending to visit places they couldn't go. But now, Steve felt as though he should treat Herobrine to the beach after this. They walked away from it, and that's when Steve and Wendy realized how small this island was. Just one small circular beach, and on the center was a patch of grass, where a straw hut stood. There was a clothesline between two trees where robes were drying off, and there was a fire pit next to that. They walked to the hut, and Elena stood in front, her knuckles politely knocking on the door.

At first, no one walked to there, but then the door swung open, and a man wearing a sparkling grey robe stood. He had long graying hair that was tied in a ponytail and a speckled beard, and he looked surprisingly fit. Steve expected a tiny old man with a long white beard, just like the stories he had read.

"Elena dear?" he asked, raising his eyebrows. "You haven't talked to me since I gave you all of those diamonds."

Elena gave him an apologetic look, and for the first time, she looked like a vulnerable woman instead of a regal lady.

"I warned you that vanity would cause you to forget about me," her father stated.

"Sorry, father. I admit the celebrity life consumed me, but these two young people need your help."

Instead of looking at Steve and Wendy, the wizard looked at Jerkin. "Is that your butler?" he asked.

Elena nodded. "This is Jerkin."

"My pleasure to meet you," Jerkin said, extending a hand. Elena's father ignored it, instead looking at Steve.

"So, what do these two want? Do they want me to make them rich as well?"

Steve shook his head. "I need you to help me to enchant my weapon. I'm being chased by this powerful cult member named Draven and—"

Elena's father's eyes widened, and then he shouted "Draven? He's still alive?"

Steve was confused, and the father wasn't giving him any more information about what was going on, instead inviting them all in. As they stepped inside, a pot was boiling tea, and it coincidentally went off once they sat at the table.

"You can call me Rara, by the way," the wizard said.

"So, who's Draven?" Wendy asked.

"It's a long story, and I'll explain in time. The fact that he's around means that there is big trouble for this world," Rara told them.

Elena scoffed. "I blew him up sky high. There's no need to worry."

"And the mansion is gone. Now who will I serve?" Jerkin lamented.

Rara shook his head. "An explosion, killing Draven? Sometimes it's hard to believe that you're my daughter due to your foolishness."

Elena looked offended while Steve had to chuckle. He thought he had family issues, but seeing them talk was as awkward as it came.

Elena scoffed. By this point, she stopped being an aristocrat and changed to an angsty daughter. "Well, sorry for not knowing about the great wizards you've fought in the past, *dad*."

Rara chose the logical option and ignored her, instead speaking to Steve.

"I'll tell you all there is to know about Draven," he told Steve.

According to Rara, most aspiring wizards went to their own schools of wizardry, which were held close to castles. Some trained to be the wizard of a king, many were put there by their own parents because someone told them that they had great magical potential, and there were a few who went because they wanted more power, whether for good, evil, or ambiguous reasons. Rara went after someone witnessed him turning dirt into sand while he was playing with it. That someone was a wizard, and Rara explained how he didn't know how he did it. As such, the wizard recommended him to attend, and so did his parents.

Rara spent most of his time in school learning about his alchemy and how to improve it. Being an alchemist was rare, and many governments dismissed the idea of them existing, so there were no laws that told merchants to analyze money and other valuables to make sure they weren't made from alchemy. While the makeup of gold was similar to gold made from alchemy, there were a few subtle differences that only an expert could detect. Before he had Elena, Rara swore that he would just use alchemy to show off and nothing more, and in the first few years, classes were going well. Until he shared a class with Draven. He was a new student, and the professor of transformative magic introduced him as a magical prodigy, claiming he had the potential to harness most magical powers. Draven told the class that he was going to be a castle wizard when he grew older, and he spoke in a meek voice, sounding like your average awkward new student. Rara, being an older student, thought it would be nice to help Draven out, to introduce him to the school and show him everything.

"At first, we clicked well together," Rara told Steve. "We had a lot in common and were best friends for a while."

"What happened then?" Wendy asked.

Rara opened his mouth to reply, but then let out a sigh, almost looking as though he could break down any second.

"I'm sorry. Just give me a few hours. I need to cope."

Steve thought that whatever happened to Rara must have been traumatizing, and although he wished that Rara would tell him more, he respected his decision. Rara walked to his bedroom while Steve talked to Elena.

"Do you know what happened?" he asked.

Elena shook her head. "My father never told me much about his past. He always seemed like the reserved type, so I never bothered asking him."

This made Steve even more curious. What could Rara hold that was such a secret?

A traveler walked across the dirt road, on his usual daily walk. His old bones were hurting as of recently, but he had to bear through the pain for the purposes of good health. He looked at the mansion ahead of him. It only was built a few years ago, and it was almost like a landmark to people. He gazed at for a few seconds, and that's when it exploded. An earth-shattering sound filled the air, knocking him back a little. Debris flew far, almost in his range. The flames danced where the mansion once stood for what appeared to be a few minutes and then began to subside.

The traveler forgot that he was seventy and began running towards the ruins. It was highly unlikely that someone had survived, but miracles did happen. He ran over the gate, which became twisted and melted from the force and heat of the explosion, and he stood upon the ruins. There appeared to be nothing left except for a few bits of diamond. Then he saw the statue in front of him. In the center of the rubble, a statue of a human stood, and it was made from complete diamond. He almost wanted to tell everyone about this, forgetting about the fact that there could have been someone inside of the mansion when it exploded.

As he stared at the statue, it almost seemed like it was moving. When he adjusted his eyes, it was revealed that there was truth to this. The diamond statue was walking towards him, and as it did, it began changing. It flawlessly transitioned from rock to flesh, and the person who stood in front of him wore a dark hood that almost looked like a dragon.

"Surprised?" the man asked. The old man had had enough. He began running away, the hooded man laughing at the ensuing hilarity.

Draven looked at the rubble. He hadn't expected this mansion to have such a booby trap. If it weren't for the fact that he could detect an incoming explosion a half-second before it destroyed everything, he wouldn't have been able to turn into diamond in time, and it would have been the end. The members he brought with him didn't seem so lucky.

Oh well, I can convert more, and besides, they're more for show in this case. I'm the one who holds the power.

He looked amongst the rubble for any signs of the boy and girl. Draven doubted that the owner of this mansion would take herself out with it. There had to be some sort of escape route they had gone into before they had activated the self-destruct, and a-ha!

Draven found a hole near where the back of the mansion once was. From the look of it, it went down a long way. A ladder led the way down, but Draven had no time for that. He jumped down the hole, turning himself into diamond. After a few seconds, he hit the ground and changed back. They wouldn't get away this time.

Chapter Two

Elena was busy comforting her father while Jerkin joined her. This led Steve and Wendy to sit outside, and that's when Wendy had a plan.

"Hey, we should go swimming at the beach while we wait for Rara to get over whatever spell he's under."

Steve's face lit up, almost as though he were a kid again. After all of the trials they'd gone through, he supposed that he should allow himself to have some fun in the sun. He nodded to Wendy, and she continued.

"I'm going inside and seeing if they have any swimwear for us to use. I'm sure that they might, and they'll probably let us use them."

"Hey, I'm down for swimming in our clothes if we have to," Steve added, and Wendy laughed as she went outside.

A few minutes passed, and then Wendy walked outside, wearing a red swimsuit that went well with her long red hair. Steve blushed a little, thinking that she looked great in it. Wendy handed Steve a pair of swimming trunks, and at first, it didn't register that Steve had to change. Then he snapped out of it, looking embarrassed, and he walked to the back of Rara's house. There, he changed, making sure that no one was looking. The trunks were a tad big, but they worked. Steve met up with Wendy, and the two walked towards the beach. When they reached the shore, they felt the wet sand teasing their feet, the waves causing them to cringe at how cold they were.

"I used to be quite the swimmer," Wendy told him. "I used to swim all around Chance, and I was told by my parents that I was going to turn into a fish if I stayed in there too long." She let out a sigh. "But when I took over the business, I stopped swimming, and I don't even know if I still have it."

Steve himself had his own few watering holes where he'd gone swimming. He remembered splashing water on Herobrine, who returned the favor by slurping the water and spitting it back at Steve. Even after Herobrine's disappearance, Steve still managed to swim, which was something that the hypnotist thankfully didn't take away. However, it had been a while for him as well.

"It's been a while for me too. Why don't we have a race to see if we still have it?" Steve suggested.

Wendy let out a grin. "Ooh, I like the sound of that."

Steve saw a rock poking form the water from a little far away. "Why don't we swim to that rock and back, and whoever does it first wins?"

Wendy grinned, a look of confidence gleaming in her eyes. "Oh, you're on. I can already feel my gills returning, and you're going to regret the day you ever challenged me."

Steve and Wendy got into position at the shore, and after they counted to three, they ran until the water became deep. Then they started swimming. Steve was self-taught for the most part when it came to swimming. As such, he swam in his own freestyle kind of way, combining many techniques, from a butterfly stroke to even dog paddling. Wendy's swimming was a consistent breaststroke that competed quite well with his. Steve had to pick up the pace, and already he was slowed down by water getting into his mouth. Unlike his swimming holes, the water here was extremely salty, and saltiness was not his favorite taste.

Steve and Wendy touched the rock at the same time, and they ended up bouncing from it and going back. Steve continued changing up his technique while Wendy chugged like an engine. The shore was getting closer, and soon both ran out of the water and jumped to the sand.

"I won!" Steve shouted.

Wendy shook her head. "I totally got there an inch before you did. It was hard to see, but I made it to the shore before you."

Steve felt his face grow red. "I'm pretty sure that I had a centimeter advantage."

The two bickered about who won for a while until they decided that they were both great at swimming. Steve offered to do a tie breaker, but Wendy said that she was beat. She reached around her hair and began squeezing the water out, her hair absorbing a lot. Water splashed all over the sand, and Steve shook his head to get more water out. They sat on the sand and looked at the ocean.

"You never realize how big life is until you look at the ocean," Wendy observed.

Steve turned to her. "That is true. I once read that most of the world is water. This planet belongs to the fish more than anything."

They looked at the ocean for a little while before Wendy stood up. "I think we should get back. Maybe he's calmed down a bit."

Steve nodded. "I just wondered what happened between him and Rara. He seemed shook up about it when we mentioned it."

Wendy scratched her head. "I wonder too. I mean, maybe we can learn Draven's true motivations. Is he serving the Ender Dragon or himself? It feels as though when one question is answered, another two pop up."

Steve agreed, and they took turns standing behind the house to change again. Their clothes were a little damp, as they hadn't brought any towels, but it would have to do. The two went back inside, and that's when Rara stood with Elena and Jerkin.

"Okay, I think I've composed myself a little better," Rara told them. "My daughter reminded me how important it is that I tell you two."

"They ruined my house, don't you know?" Elena commented. Steve and Wendy facepalmed.

Rara opened his mouth again and was about to begin his story, and that's when a sound was heard from outside of the house. It sounded like an explosion.

Immediately, Rara ran outside, the rest of them following. When Steve and Wendy saw what Rara was looking at, their jaws dropped.

Draven stood at the shore, the building that took them to the tunnel in ruins. A grin spread around his face as he undid his hood. He looked at Rara in particular, and he began to laugh.

"My, my. It looks as though the Ender Dragon really is the controller of fate. Not only do I find the heroes again, but also I find Rara. I thought you were dead to the world."

Rara shook his head, and suddenly a look of anger grew around his face. "Draven, how many times do you have to be told? There is no such thing as an Ender Dragon, and to believe in such fairy tales at your age is preposterous!"

Steve wanted to tell him that the Ender Dragon was, in fact, real. But now was not the time. Draven began laughing.

"Oh please," he replied. "The Ender Dragon has already been resurrected. Just ask the boy over here, and you'll know all about it."

Rara looked at Steve with a concerned look, and all Steve said was, "I'll tell you later. Right now, we need to get out of here. He's too dangerous."

Rara stared back to Draven, who still grinned. "See, I told you. The Ender Dragon is very real, and when he comes, I'll make sure that you're his next meal. Now, I've destroyed your way out, and there's obviously not a boat around. We can do this the easy way, or we can do it the hard way. Either way is up to—"

All of a sudden, Draven shot out projectiles of ice that was sharper than swords. They headed towards Rara, but before they could hit him, he stuck out his palm. Suddenly, the ice melted, leaving water to splash on his face.

"You were always about surprise attacks," Rara said. "You didn't think that I would not know that?"

Draven shot out a few more projectiles, all of which were in different elements. Rara melted ice, turned fire into harmless embers, a blast of wind into a light breeze, and turned rock into soft clay. Steve noticed that Rara never destroyed the projectiles, but instead turned them into something harmless.

"Curse you," Draven yelled, and suddenly his body turned to diamond. He then charged towards Rara, and just as he was about to strike, Rara stuck out his hands. Draven's body suddenly changed to a dirt body, and before Rara could make him crumble, Draven turned back to normal.

"Ha, your magic has most certainly improved. However, I've been saving my best attack for last, and I believe that not even your strongest magic can damage me while I'm in this form."

Draven appeared as though he was concentrating hard, and before Rara could attack, Draven's body began to change into a grayish hue, almost blackened. Steve remembered reading about it in a mineral book with his brother, Herobrine, and a shiver went down his spine. Wendy, an expert on mines, began gasping.

"Say, big brother, do you really think that bedrock is indestructible?" Herobrine asked him.

Steve read a book on minerals to Herobrine, and they got to the chapter where they talked about bedrock. According to the book, bedrock was a mineral that was said to hold the land, and you could not destroy it. Diamond, lava, even obsidian all felt like a poke in the cheek to bedrock, and the fun facts in the book mentioned that a rich daredevil once spent his fortune on buying enough TNT to cover a city, trying to get enough destructive power to crack into the bedrock. The explosion didn't scratch the bedrock, and the man was arrested for destroying a good chunk of land.

"I'd like to find out. Maybe Dad can destroy it with his big feet," Steve suggested, and the two giggled.

"I bet Mom could break it with her big butt," Herobrine replied, and the earth shook from their laughter. Their parents came in wondering what was so funny, but they never found out.

It was interesting how good nostalgic memories came back after something so traumatizing was going on. Now Draven was made from bedrock, and when he walked, he moved at a surprisingly fast pace.

Rara looked afraid now, and he turned around and started panicking.

"There's no way we can defeat him. However, I have a potion in my house that will grant me temporary teleportation powers. This way, we can escape," he said.

"You can't zap him into another dimension like you said you would to those creeps that followed me at school?" Elena asked.

Rara shook his head. "Now is not the time for jokes. Let's run."

They made it inside of the hut, and bedrock Draven waved his hands at the door, destroying everything in his path. Before they knew it, the house was crumbling behind them, and as they ran into Rara's bedroom, they wondered if they'd be in a pile of rubble before Rara found the potions. The door broke open, and Draven stood, the ceiling above them about to collapse.

"Found it," Rara declared, and he drank the potion, running back to the group. Draven approached them, ready to slap their heads off with his bedrock hands. Before his hand could come down, however, they disappeared.

They reappeared in a field, and in front of them was what appeared to be an old castle. The bricks were crumbling, and vines grew along its walls. A watchtower stood on the center, going up so high until it stopped, apparently broke off or unfinished.

Steve and Wendy looked at this building in awe. Elena and Jerkin thought that the castle could use some cleanup.

"I highly doubt Draven would think that I would come back to the academy," he told them. Steve was in awe. The castle didn't look like an academy at all.

Chapter Three

The interior of the academy was covered in cobwebs as far as the eye could see. Steve realized that once, this place probably looked like a prestigious university. He could see remnants of what appeared to be colorful carpet, faded paintings of all of the founding members, and empty rooms with a few chairs inside. They crashed in one of those rooms, setting up a circle of chairs that they sat at. Rara made everyone comfortable as he began his story.

Draven and Rara clicked well together, and as the school year went on, their bonds became stronger. Draven was a frail student, and since magic use was forbidden to use except for in the classrooms, he had a hard time dealing with bullies who were bigger than him and thought that he was a freak. The school had a spell on it to where even if you wanted to use magic, you couldn't unless the wizards instructed you to do so. That meant that they had to fight physically, and Draven couldn't do that. Rara wasn't much of a fighter, either, but he managed to stand up to the bullies long enough for them to go away.

Rara didn't get why everyone hated Draven; he was reserved, but once you go to know him, he seemed nice. A bit awkward at times, but a good heart all around. Draven grew trusting of Rara, and come the next school year, Draven wanted to be roommates with Rara. Rara accepted, knowing that he would be a much more chill roommate than his obnoxious one from last year. Becoming a teenager was already annoying, and he didn't want someone to pester him all throughout the year.

Now that they lived together, Rara noticed that Draven was gone a lot. Occasionally, he left when they were hanging out, but Rara assumed that he was going back to his room to study. This was their room, so shouldn't Draven be studying in here? Also, Draven became quiet over the months, keeping to himself, even at the cost of alienating his friend. He was usually open with Rara and no one else, but now Rara felt as though Draven was ignoring even him.

Wondering what he was up to, Rara decided to follow him one night. He was not the type to poke his nose into other people's lives, but something about Draven's behavior seemed off. Besides the shyness, he seemed shaken, almost as though he'd gone through a traumatic experience.

When Draven got up to leave, Rara waited a few minutes and then followed him down the hallway, trying to move as lightly as he could. Rara saw him go down the corridor and down the stairs, and eventually he walked to the main hallway. The double doors stood in front of him, and Rara wondered what Draven was doing. At night, the quarters were closed with magic so that no student could get out, so how was Draven getting out?

"Ender Aloan Ender Paha!"

These words came from Draven's mouth, and it almost sounded like a chant of sorts. When he uttered those words, the doors opened. Rara had his mouth open in fear. Didn't the academy prevent magic from being used? So how was Draven able to do that? Perhaps a fine wizard could break the spell, but Draven, the weakling who was bullied?

Rara followed Draven outside of the academy, where the moon shined with fullness, not a single cloud in the sky. Rara hid behind trees, giant rocks, and under tall grass to prevent his cover from being blown. It was essential that he didn't get caught after going so far. This was getting deep, and Rara had to know how deep the hole really went. Was Draven just an outdoors person who dug the fresh air, or was there something more sinister afoot?

Soon, he found his answer. Draven went over a hill, and under it was a pit of fire. People had gathered around it, all wearing cloaks that resembled that of the Ender Dragon, a legend that was told to the school in mythology class. Draven spoke to the leader of the group, a stern-faced man.

"How goes it?" the man asked. "I haven't asked about your school in a while."

Draven had a serious look in his face all this time, but suddenly it changed to match the Draven whom Rara knew. "Oh, it's going great, Father. I made a new friend and—"

Smack!

Draven's father's hand went across Draven's face, knocking the boy back and leaving behind a mark. At this point in his life, Draven had hit his growth spurt and was taller than his father, so why didn't Draven stand up for himself.

The stern-faced man grew even sterner. "I told you that this academy is not for making friends. You're supposed to be mastering your magic skills and trying to form connections so that one day you can rule the academy and recruit our children for the upcoming return of the Ender Dragon!"

The members surrounding the two cringed at this site, and so did Rara. The return of the Ender Dragon? He knew that apparently there were people who believed the story to be true and waited for its return, but he didn't expect in a million years that Draven, the awkward boy he thought he knew, would be one who believed this. Though, from the look of it, his father was instilling the idea in him.

After that, they performed rituals, and the group was dismissed. Draven walked back, looking down. Rara managed to get back to the academy before he returned, its doors still opened by Draven breaking the spell. When Draven returned, Rara wanted to confront him about what he'd seen, but Draven ended up falling asleep as soon he went back to his room, Rara not wanting to tell him about what had happened. He could barely sleep that night.

Rara hid the fact that he'd experienced Draven with his cult for a good while, until he couldn't take it anymore. He hated the idea of keeping something bottled up, and over the past few days, Draven's condition had worsened to the point where he could barely talk to Rara.

Just as soon as Draven was about to leave, Rara stopped him.

"Where are you going?" he asked.

Draven, who was usually calm, seemed to get aggressive, his eyes almost flaring. "I'm taking a walk around the quarters. I hate being cramped up in a space for too long."

"Oh, you're not going to go meet up with an Ender Dragon cult and get slapped by your father?" Rara asked in a condescending manner. Suddenly, Draven stood still before he finally spoke. This time, his voice was sinister. It was no longer the meek Draven that Rara was used to.

"You dare mock the Order of the Ender Dragon? I hope that it devours you once it resurrects," he told Rara.

Rara stood there, mortified. It was as though Draven had two personalities, and the bad one showed its face for the first time. Rara almost wanted to slap Draven, but felt pity towards him. It wasn't the fault of him but the people who raised him that way.

"First off, there's no such thing as an Ender Dragon. It's a myth, a fairy tale just to inspire children. Second, you tell your best friend that you wish that a dragon would devour him? You do realize how brutal that death would be. If its teeth don't tear me apart, then I'd have to watch myself turn to goo in its digestive system," Rara told Draven this in a casual, almost informative, manner, and for a second, it almost seemed as though Draven was getting it. He gazed at Rara, almost to ask what he was doing with his life. For a few seconds, he was back to the innocent Draven that Rara once knew.

Then, Draven's eyes flared up, and they almost appeared to glow. He began to pant, and when he spoke, it was deep and malicious.

"No. Such. Thing? You don't realize what you've just said. Not only do you know my secret, but you have blasphemed the name of the Ender Dragon. I joined this school just so I could get a magic degree and potentially become a high-ranking wizard for a castle, but since someone knows about me, and to prevent anyone else from knowing, since obviously you told everyone, I'm going to destroy this place!"

Before Rara could do anything, Draven shot a flurry of projectiles towards him. It was high-ranking magic, but Rara was skilled enough in magic to lessen the attacks, at first forgetting that he could even use magic, since the school usually prevented it. The fireballs he shot made exploding noises, and this caused the school to go into chaos. People woke up, and as Rara was busy neutralizing Draven's attacks, a professor opened the door to see what was going on. Immediately, Draven shot a bolt of lightning out of his finger, and the professor countered. This gave Rara enough time to escape from his room. As he ran, he heard an explosion. Draven had overpowered the professor and was coming for Rara. Draven managed to get out of the area, sprinting down the stairs. The other students tried holding Draven back, but they could not. Draven's magic overpowered them, and the place began to catch fire.

As Draven chased Rara, Rara didn't know what to do. He turned around to cast his own spell, and that's when he saw Draven encased in stone. Had someone cast a stone spell and ended this madness? Then the stone began to move, and Rara figured out that Draven had done it to himself. Rara tried using this to his advantage, but his alchemy powers were too weak. Rara had to retreat, dodging Draven's attacks. Every time Draven missed, he ended up destroying a wall or a student.

Eventually, Rara ran outside, and that's when Draven stepped outside and changed back to his normal form.

"Now, it's time to finish this, and—"

Draven suddenly grabbed his own forehead. His eyes stopped gleaming for just a second, and when he spoke, it was in the Draven-whom-Rara-knew's voice.

"I'm trying to hold him back! I have no time to explain, but get out of here as fast as you can! He'll lose interest eventually, as he only cares about resurrecting the Ender Dragon. Quickly!"

Rara had no choice. He began running, and since that day, you could say that he'd been running a long time.

Rara sighed. "I think I could have done so much to help save him. There's a good person inside of him, but it looks as though something is controlling him. The school closed down after this incident, and they never found Draven. I eventually taught myself magic, getting married and having a kid. We moved to the island, with her wanting sunshine and me wanting seclusion. Draven still frightened me and haunted my dreams, and it looks as though he's come back to haunt me in person."

Steve could empathize with him. In many respects, Draven was like Herobrine. A good person was inside of them, but evil used their bodies as vessels, and unless Steve could save them, there was no way that evil was going anywhere.

"So, what should we do?" Elena asked.

Rara looked at her and Jerkin. "I advise you two to get out now. There's a town close by, and you should be safe there." He looked at Steve. "Right now, I need to enchant a sword for you."

"No," Elena refused. "I must stay and get revenge on those who destroyed my home."

Jerkin tugged on her sleeve. "Not if I can help it. Let's go while we still can."

Elena protested, but Jerkin dragged her outside.

Meanwhile Steve almost forgot about his original purpose for coming. He wanted Rara to enchant a weapon for him, but Steve didn't even have a sword on him, since he'd lost it after Draven destroyed it. How could Steve get his weapon no—

Suddenly, Rara had a diamond sword in his hand. He had no pockets or sheath to carry it in, so how did he have it?

"I also have mastered the art of weapon summoning," Rara told Steve.

"Weapon summoning?" Steve replied.

"My weapons are locked up where no one can see them. If I need to summon a sword, I teleport that weapon from my place to my hand. It's a weaker teleportation magic, so anyone can learn it, but it's hard to master." He handed Steve the sword. Steve took it with pride.

"Now then, let me enchant the sword. There should be an enchanting book somewhere."

Chapter Four

They followed Rara deeper into the abandoned academy until they walked inside of a library with tables inside of it. The tables contained broken and intact vials, some still containing strange potions. Rara laid the sword on the table while he looked for the book that he needed. Finally, he found it. *Enchanting Weapons With Alchemy,* it read.

Rara stood in front of the sword and placed his hand on the scabbard. He began to chant, and the sword started to glow. When Rara was done, the sword stopped.

"What did that do?" Steve asked.

"I passed some of my alchemic powers to the sword. If you think about an element while attacking another element, it will change that element. Try it."

Steve grabbed the sword and slapped the table with its blade, thinking about dirt. All of a sudden, the wooden table changed to dirt in a blink of an eye.

"Wow!" Wendy declared. "Just imagine how easy it would be to run my business if I had that sword."

Rara smiled. "Well, it takes quite some experience to change it to a stronger element. I had trouble turning rocks into diamonds for quite a while until my daughter annoyed me to the point where I accidentally did it."

"So, will it work on bedrock?" Steve asked.

Rara shook his head. "Alas, I've tried to change bedrock to something weaker for many years, and not even I could do it. If he turns to bedrock, I'm certain that you can't defeat him. Although . . ."

"What?" Steve asked.

"I don't know much about body changing, but from what I've heard, it exerts a lot of energy, and the stronger element you turn yourself into, the more energy it requires. If bedrock transformation takes a lot of energy, then if you evade his attacks for long enough, he will change back."

For Steve, this sounded impossible. Draven was a powerful wizard who had seemingly all of the energy in the world. He doubted that it would take a minute for him to change back.

"So now what do we do?" Wendy asked.

"Well, I'm going to stay with you two. I need to fight Draven and face my demons. Maybe I can convince him to return to his normal self. Although, since he's been like this for decades, I doubt that the Draven I once knew is—"

"Stop," Steve interrupted. "He is in there. If he is lost, then so is my brother."

"Your brother?" Rara asked.

Steve realized that he hadn't told Rara about what had happened and why he was involved with Draven in the first place. Right then, his words started to spill, and Wendy chimed in, telling her side of the story too. Rara seemed skeptical at first but then started to believe him when Steve mentioned how Herobrine drank the blood of the Ender Dragon.

"I heard a legend from a traveler about people claiming to have Ender Dragon's blood," Rara said.

After the story was all over, Rara looked at Steve with sympathy in his eyes. "Now I know we need to stop Draven. He's the key to finding your brother and also the key so that I can have peace," he said.

Steve nodded. Herobrine was still inside of that Ender Dragon, and although he wouldn't be able to free himself, Steve knew that there was still hope of him rescuing Herobrine.

"So now where do we go?" Wendy asked, a rephrase of her last question.

"I don't even know at this point," Steve replied. "However, it almost seems as though fate always has something in store for us. We try to figure out what to do, and sure enough, we find the next step. I don't think it's going to fail us n—"

A creaking sound was heard from the distance. A chill collectively spread down the three's spines. Someone was going in the academy, and Steve peeked out of the door to see who it was.

The white face poked out in the darkness. It was none other than Draven.

Steve ran back inside and whispered to Rara.

"I thought that you said Rara wouldn't come here."

Rara sighed. "I hoped he wouldn't come, but I guess deep down, I knew he would."

"Well, what should we do?" Wendy asked.

They looked around for some place to hide, and they found an empty bookshelf with a space big enough for them to squeeze under. They squeezed, and eventually they heard the sound of footsteps entering.

"Come out, heroes! I know you're here. All you need to do is show yourself, and I'll make it painless."

Steve's heart began to beat quickly as the footsteps came closer. Soon Draven stood in front of the bookshelf, and they heard him cackling.

"An empty shelf. I guess it fits this academy, huh?"

Wendy and Steve were keeping quiet, but Rara began panting. "I'll show you!" he shouted and pushed in front of him.

The bookshelf came falling down, crashing on top of Draven. The three jumped out, and sure enough, Draven was pinned under there, seeing stars for only a second. However, this bought them enough time for them to run outside of the room. Just then, Draven cast a spell, and the bookshelf exploded into splinters. He ran out the door, shouting their names. The three thought about exiting the academy, but the door that was the entrance was barred shut, Rara claiming that Draven had sealed it.

They ran up a flight of stairs, and that's when Draven caught up to them. He began casting spells, and Rara began neutralizing them.

"Get out of here!" he told them. "I'll hold him off."

"But Rara," Steve began.

"No buts. Just go. I'll follow."

Steve and Wendy ran up the stairs and through another empty corridor, and then they encountered a set of twisting stairs. They ran up it and made it to the top, where they were led outside on the roof. The roof itself looked rotted and had moss growing on it.

Rara ran up the stairs. He sweated buckets, and his clothes were frayed. Shortly after, Draven followed suit and began throwing spells. Rara began blocking them, but from the look of it, he wasn't going to hold out for too much longer.

Steve took out his sword and decided to attack Draven from behind. If he could attack while Draven was distracted, it would be the end for the sorcerer. He ran to the side, Draven distracted, and then Steve ran towards Draven's behind. He began slashing, and that's when Draven's body turned to diamond. "Hah, did you think you were going to—"

"Go away, you piece of *dirt*," Steve shouted, and his sword went down on Draven's back. Suddenly, he turned to a figure of dirt. Before Draven could do anything, Steve attacked his arm. With one slash, Draven's arm fell off, turned into a pile of dirt, and then disappeared. Draven shouted in pain, and that's when he shifted to his bedrock form.

A hole was where Draven's arm was, and for a second, he could see something inside. Almost as if there was an orb of light inside of Draven, ready to come out. Steve ran towards the wound and was ready to jam his sword in there, but something stopped him. Another arm appeared where Draven's arm had been cut off, regenerating in a matter of seconds. The bedrock arm swung towards Steve and Steve had little time to defend. He jumped out of the way, and Draven turned back to him.

"Ugh, you've been the best fight I've had in a long time. But when I'm in my bedrock stage, I am invincible. I can regenerate, and nothing can penetrate this body."

Steve swung his sword and hit Draven on the chest, wanting him to turn back into dirt. Even diamond, if that was the best he could do. However, the bedrock did not budge. Draven shot a projectile out of his arm, and Steve jumped out of the way while Draven cackled. Rara kept attacking, but it was not hurting Draven whatsoever.

Panting, Rara deflected the next round of projectiles. He appeared to be on his last rope. While Draven attacked, he fired one projectile towards the stairs leading downwards. *Boom!* They crumbled, and there was no way down. This startled Rara enough to give an opening, and Draven lunged towards Rara.

Bam!

Draven's fist sank into Rara's stomach, knocking the wind out of him and causing him to collapse. Steve and Wendy rushed to his aid as Rara laughed.

"D-D-Draven," Rara croaked. A bit of blood seeped from his mouth as he said this. When Draven looked at him, he stopped laughing. His skin changed back from bedrock to flesh, and he had a look of concern on his face. He almost looked childlike, having the appearance of a kid who had done something wrong.

"Rara?" he asked, his tears coming out fast. "What did they make me do to you?"

Draven fell on his knees, and Steve could have finished it. But he realized that the real Draven came out, and he was not about to hurt an innocent man.

Rara cracked a smile, despite the fact that he seemed to be losing the grip on his life. "You've been taken over by evil. But no more. You should fight against this Ender Dragon, not for it. That's all I wanted to tell you when we were kids. Start your own path in life. Both of us aren't spring chickens, but it's never too late to change the path you're on."

Draven started crying. "I'm so sorry. My father gave me the Bile of the Ender Dragon when I was a child. It gave me great powers for the expense of losing my mind. I'm sorry for all I have done, but I can't do anything about it now. I've fatally hurt my best friend, my only friend. I don't know what to do about myself."

"Please," Steve told Draven. "You have to fight it. You're the master of your own life, no one else. Not even a force inside of you can do anything about it."

"I guess," Draven replied.

Steve let out a sigh of relief. Although he wasn't sure about Rara's condition, it appeared as though Draven had snapped out of it and was going to pull himself together. Maybe he could use his magic to heal Rara.

"But you don't understand," Draven continued. "When one is chosen to be the Claw of the Ender, opting out is not an option. You just can't- *shut up!*"

All of a sudden, Draven shot out a projectile. It appeared to be a ball of dark energy that pulsated, and it struck Rara.

Rara disappeared entirely.

"What!" Wendy shouted in disbelief.

"How could you do something like that?" Steve added.

When Draven spoke, he sounded back to his old self. "Ahh, it's been a while since he interrupted my duties. But never the matter; I've suppressed him for good this time." Draven walked towards the two. "And now, I'm going to finish you two off."

Chapter Five

Steve and Wendy avoided the projectiles of Draven as he fired a slew of fireballs. However, there was little room on the roof, and Draven kept inching closer, eventually getting right next to the two of them. He swung his fists, and they ducked. Then he kicked at them. Steve pulled Wendy aside, and they got out of the way but for how long?

The only option is to get out of here and think of a plan, but how? The only way down is to jump off, and we're probably going to break our legs if we do that, Steve thought.

They stood on the edge, wondering what they were going to do.

"Now to finish this!" Draven shouted, and he swung his hands.

Suddenly, two small beads hit the ground close to Draven, and before he could do anything, they exploded in a cloud of smoke. Draven shouted, not being able to see anything, and Steve and Wendy got out of the way. Someone had saved them, but who?

"You two again, huh? I didn't think I'd ever see you, much less saving your butts."

Someone stood on the center of the roof, and Steve's jaw dropped as he saw who it was.

The ponytail had been chopped off, leaving a mess of shaggy blond hair, and now he dressed more like an explorer, with a belt filled with gadgets to boot. But that cocky look on his face made Steve recognize him immediately. It was Bartholomew.

Bartholomew had been a thief who robbed from Wendy with his gang of thieves on his side. Steve infiltrated their hideout and thought that he had defeated Bartholomew, but the thief came back and swore vengeance on Steve until Steve promised him the treasure from the city of Chance's castle once he had defeated Herobrine. When that didn't happen, Bartholomew let him go anyway after everything went down, and he said that he was considering going straight or at least more honestly. Steve couldn't tell which path Bartholomew was on right now, but it was definitely a change.

Wendy gasped at Bartholomew, but she left her grudge at the door. Right now, Bartholomew was saving their skin. Bartholomew threw two more smoke bombs, blinding Draven enough for him to grab Steve and Wendy. They held on to his shoulders as he declared, "Hold on tight."

Bartholomew took out a strange gadget from his belt. A few yards away, there was a tree, but it was out of reach. Bartholomew pointed the gadget at the tree diagonally until it pointed near its trunk and fired. All of a sudden, a grapple shot out and impaled the trunk. Bartholomew, Steve, and Wendy flew off the roof and towards the tree, and in midair; Bartholomew took out another grapple and shot a lower section of the tree. Their fall was broken, they flew towards the tree, and they fell safely to the ground. Bartholomew discarded the grapples and they began to run, far gone from Draven by the time he recovered.

When they reached a safe place, they began to talk.

"How did you know we were here? Steve asked.

"Been stalking us?" Wendy quipped.

"Well, I told Steve that I was considering going straight or being honest. Well, living a life with a normal nine-to-five job wasn't the idea for me, but I decided to be more honest, and I became an explorer. I built these gadgets myself, and I've currently been exploring ruins, dungeons, caves, and mines. I've actually bagged a lot more than when I was a thief. I heard about this abandoned magic academy and how there are many passages that people have been speculating are undiscovered, so I decided to see if there was anything of value. Instead, I saw you all fighting, so I grappled to the roof."

"Thanks for that," Steve replied. "We owe you one. And you seem less cocky now, so that's a plus."

"Hey, I'm still Bartholomew the Great, but now I'm a great explorer instead of a great thief. Also, we still haven't settled our score."

"I thought you had gone honest," Steve replied.

"I have, but I still want to fight. I suppose it can wait, though. Who was that guy?"

Steve and Wendy explained what all had happened, and even Bartholomew thought it was shocking. "He killed his friend and almost killed you two," he stated.

Steve nodded, feeling glum about Rara's death. Of course, did he really die? He supposed that it was the denial part of his mine wishing for something that wasn't true, but the idea of Rara still being alive but captured by Draven gave him hope.

"He's going to pay," Wendy said.

"But how? From the look of it, he was bedrock, and you can't destroy bedrock."

"There might be a way," Steve stated.

Wendy looked at him.

"When I cut off his arm, I thought I saw something glowing from inside the hole. I think it's the core of his power, where the good Draven is being held. If I could get to that after cutting an opening, then maybe I could defeat him."

"You sure?" Wendy asked.

"I mean, it's all speculative, but I have a hunch that it's a key source of his power. If I could just get him once while he wasn't in his bedrock state, then maybe we could defeat him. The real Draven is inside, and we should not make Rara's sacrifice be in vain."

They all nodded, even Bartholomew.

"I guess you can go now," Wendy told him. "Thanks for your help."

Bartholomew shook his head. "I'm interested in taking out this creep as well. There is probably something valuable connected with the Ender Dragon, and I can't wait to get my hands on it."

Steve sighed, knowing that deep down, Bartholomew was the same old Bartholomew, but he was at least a bit more charming this time around.

They eventually ran into a castle town, which was not as big as Chance but still sizable enough. They were able to pass the two guards, who let them into the gates. Apparently, they made it in the nick of time, as they closed the gates after sunset.

It was a small enough town so that they could find an inn rather fast, and sure enough, there were two rooms available. Steve and Wendy got their own room while Bartholomew got his, and before they went into the rooms, they saw a familiar face.

It was Elena, looking glummer than before.

"What's wrong?" Steve asked.

"Jerkin left. As regal as he looks, he's actually a beggar who I hired because I felt bad for him. As soon as he realized that he was in a larger town and that I probably won't be rich for a good while, he left to beg."

Steve didn't know what to do. He didn't want to tell her about her father's death while she was in this condition, but lying wasn't his strong suit.

"By the way, where's my father?" she asked.

"We ran into Draven after you left. He attacked us, and we got separated from him."

Elena looked at him with skeptical eyes. "You don't have to play dumb with me. If my father was killed, just spill it. I'm a big girl." She sighed. "I know he had a demon to face, and if he died doing that, then he should be able to rest easy.

"Actually, I don't know. Draven attacked him and hurt him badly, but then used a spell to make him disappear."

"Disappear? I've never heard of a death spell doing that. Even the obliterating spells leave behind ashes. He's probably still out there, and knowing him, he'll pull through."

Elena still seemed broken, but she looked as though she would deal with it for now. Steve and Wendy went to their room while Bartholomew went to his. Inside, Wendy and Steve took separate showers, the hot water relieving them of their sorrows, and before they went to bed, they talked about what had happened.

"Steve, I've been through a lot with you. I've watched you get thrown off a waterfall, I've been kidnapped, we've survived being almost executed, so I know we can pull through this. I know we can take down the Claw of the Ender and eventually the Ender Dragon himself."

Steve nodded. "But even Herobrine seemed vulnerable. Draven's attacks make him nearly invincible except for that one weak spot. If I can attack that in time, maybe I'll win, but it needs to perfect, and—"

Before he could finish his sentence, Wendy rushed up to Steve and kissed him lightly on the mouth. They held that kiss for a few seconds before Wendy pulled away, blushing. Steve was in awe. He had never been kissed before, and he considered Wendy to be just a friend to him. However, he blushed, and Wendy's cheeks grew as red as her hair.

"That's in case if we don't make it the next time we fight Draven."

He found himself back in the castle tower, and he was cursing himself as he returned. He had lost those brats again thanks to this mysterious third person, and even though he banished his sworn enemy to spend eternity in The End, he felt as though he hadn't accomplished anything.

Draven sat down on his bed, and that's when he had a feeling in his gut. The Ender Dragon was almost about to reawaken, and when it did, the dragon would be unimpressed in the cult that Draven had formed. Most had perished, and too many people didn't believe those tales anyway.

As he opened his window and looked down on the city, he had another feeling in his gut as well. Those heroes, they were in this town. He could go to where they were, probably the inn, and kill them without the town noticing. They wouldn't want to see their wizard turn out to be a baddie, after all. But he wasn't going to do that just yet. He knew that the Ender Dragon was angry, and he had a last chance to show the dragon what he could do. This was the final showdown before the beginning of the end. The Ender Dragon was coming, and Draven had to give him the welcoming party of a lifetime. There in the next few days, there was going to be blood, and Draven couldn't wait for it to happen. As he went to sleep, he felt a nagging sensation in his mind. The boy was still trying to break free, but this was an aging adult's body now, and there was no way he was coming back. The only thing that was going to return was the Ender Dragon.

Meanwhile, Steve couldn't sleep. He looked outside his window, and he had a feeling that something was about to go down soon. He saw Wendy sleeping soundly on the bed next to him, and this made him sigh. Wendy had more or less told him that she had feelings for him, and now that Steve thought about it, so did he. When this was all over, Steve wouldn't mind bringing not only his brother home to his parents, but a girl named Wendy as well. However, he still feared for her. He brought her into this mess, and the idea that something could happen to her scared him. He knew that she wouldn't leave this train no matter how many times he asked, however. So as he gripped his enchanted sword, he knew that he had to make the next fight he had matter. Not only for Draven's sake so that he could be free, but also for Wendy, the girl that he liked. The Ender Dragon wasn't going to take away any of these people. It had taken too many already, and Steve planned on putting a stop to it.

The Cult, Part Three

Chapter One

Steve and Wendy stepped out of their inn and decided to explore the castle town a bit. While they were wondering where they were going to go and when Draven would strike next, they realized that they didn't even know anything about the place they had ended up at.

"This is the castle town of Ende," one of the merchants told them before trying to sell them a potion that looked like a vial of colored water. They passed him up and continued walking.

While they did this, they kept awkwardly holding their hands before letting them go. Bartholomew didn't answer when they knocked on his door and Elena was grieving over the apparent loss of her father, so it was just the two of them, but the tension was still high. Steve knew that he was in love with Wendy, and the feeling was mutual. But something preventing them from going full-on lovers.

Maybe it's just the stress of Draven, he thought. *Once we get rid of him and defeat the Ender Dragon, then we can be boyfriend and girlfriend.* The idea of a girlfriend excited him, as he had never had one. He knew that the stakes were higher when it came to protecting Wendy, and because of this, he promised not to let her go.

Ende was built similarly to Chance, but was less populated and smaller, thus making it easier to navigate. So far, they didn't see any sign of Draven or any of his lackeys. Everyone looked chill and went about with their day. If Draven was here, half of the town would be in flames, and there would be bodies piled up all over the streets. The thought of that made Steve shudder as they went further.

They saw the castle overlooking them. While not as grand as Chance's, it still had dignity to it.

"Do you think we lost him?" Wendy asked after they passed by the town's fountain. This one was a statue of an Enderman, water pouring from its limbs.

"He's like a cockroach. We tried blowing him up, and that didn't work. We tried teleporting, but he found us. I don't think running away will do anything."

Wendy sighed and they sat down on the edge of the fountain. Upon further examination, a plaque rested under the statue. "THE END MIGHT JUST BE THE BEGINNING," it read. "DONATED BY THE WIZARD VRADNE," was inscribed below.

"Just what does that even mean?" Steve asked.

Wendy shook her head. "Don't ask me. Probably just something pretentious. You know how stuck-up some of the castle wizards are."

"No I don't. Did Chance even have a castle wizard?"

"We once did. He passed a few years ago, and since then, Chance couldn't find a wizard worthy enough to be his successor. If we had one, maybe Herobrine wouldn't have taken over."

Steve sighed, thinking about his brother's name, and Wendy understood. Despite the tranquility of where they sat, Steve's nerves were still shot. He wondered if Draven knew about Steve and Wendy's relationship. If so, would he try to use that to his advantage? Draven might try kidnapping her, or worse...

"Steve, are you okay?" Wendy asked.

"I'm fine. I'm just thinking."

"I know that Draven can attack any minute, but let's relax for a bit. We're in a new town, so who knows what we can find."

Steve nodded. "True."

"Besides that, I highly doubt that he would attack us in a busy place such as this. Draven is powerful, but he's not stupid enough to have an entire army on him."

"Maybe, but you never know. He's ruthless, so it wouldn't be out of character for him to strike now."

They soon stood up and continued to look around. A clown stood at the corner and juggled flaming balls, much to the amusement of the children watching him. Two adults gossiped over the happenings of Chance.

"My cousin lives there and he said that the king was actually a reptile," one said to the other.

"Oh please. That just sounds like a huge conspiracy theory. Yet again, sometimes I feel like the ones in power aren't human."

Steve wanted to join in, but instead ignored them. If Draven was in this town, the last thing he needed was for them to be noticed. While Draven would probably see them immediately if he was around, he could be asking other people about their location.

They went near the castle, and from their vantage point, they noticed its gates were open, and the people could come and go as they pleased. Unlike Chance, where the gates were sealed once Herobrine took over.

"Want to go in the castle?" Steve asked.

"I don't see why not," Wendy replied.

They walked past the gates, where the guards gave them an uncaring glance, and they climbed up a series of stone stairs until they reached the very top. They saw the doors to the castle and walked inside, with Steve noticing that a tower stood close by. It was separate from the castle and guards stood at the entrance. Inside, the hallway looked grand enough with paintings of old kings and gold decorations everywhere, and with a few guards stationed around to make sure that no one stole anything. According to a sign in front of them, the castle opened its doors to the public once a month, and today just happened to be their lucky day.

As they walked down a corridor, a child was bawling his eyes out, her mother trying to calm her down, but with no avail.

"Don't worry. I'm sure he's just sick. He'll come out later to play with you."

The kid just cried further. "There's no way that a wizard could get sick! He just doesn't like me!" With that, they left the area and a guard close by decided to make small talk with them.

"Usually, the castle wizard Vradne keeps his tower opened for a meet and greet with all of the children and magic lovers who want to see him, but this is the first time that he's shut his tower down. He told us that he wants to be left alone. It's so unusual."

"Why's that?" Steve asked.

"Because Vradne usually lets anyone talk to him on the days when the castle is open to the public. He's never been ill and he certainly didn't sound ill from the look of it."

"Why doesn't the king make him?" Wendy asked.

"The wishes of the castle wizard are just as important, if not more so, than the desires of the king. Because of that, no one wants to force him to do anything."

"Understandable," Wendy replied.

They explored around the castle a little more, even running into the king at one point. He looked like your stereotypical benevolent king. He was slightly chubby, had a flowing gray beard, and made a hearty laugh at everything that was even remotely funny. They soon left and wondered where their next destination would be.

"Want to go check up on Elena, or see if Bartholomew is up?" Steve asked.

"I'm certainly worried about Elena, but I'm not sure if Bartholomew was even sleeping. Knowing him, he's probably lurking around somewhere. I can't believe how much he's changed, though. As much as I despise him, he's an alright guy now. And I'm not saying that just because he saved our skins."

She looked at Steve. "And I think that you're the reason why. You showed him how life wasn't about stealing from others, and that caused him to live a cleaner life."

"Do you really think it was because of me?" Steve asked.

She nodded. "You change people for the better. I've never felt more alive despite all that has happened, after all."

This gave Steve some assurance. He was down because of everything that had happened. Because of him, his brother was a dragon, Rara was either dead or sealed in an alternate world, and Elena was fatherless and homeless. Not to mention that he was responsible for a village burning down. Granted, most of those things were caused by Draven, but Steve felt some guilt. It was like having a virus and spreading it to people even though you realized how contagious it was.

Steve smiled. "Thanks Wendy. I needed that." He extended out his hand, and they held hands.

On the way back to the inn, they came across a few alleyways. Feeling adventurous, they decided to go explore a few of them. They consisted of stinking garbage and old flyers, the latter they found interesting. There was an advertisement for a juggling competition, a singing event, and more. However, the alley led to a dead end.

"Come on, let's get out of here," Steve said, and they turned back, looking at one last glance of the fliers. That was when one caught his eye. He told Wendy to look at it, and they both gasped.

It was a poster for a magic show by Vradne the wizard. It contained the details, which didn't raise eyebrows, but most of the flier contained an illustration of Vradne's face.

"Doesn't this face look like Draven?" Steve asked.

"It does! I mean, this guy's smiling and looks genuinely happy, but his face looks just like Draven's, and he has the same hair as well.

"Maybe it's just a coincidence. I mean, this is a drawing. Maybe he doesn't look like this, and someone botched it to the point where he looks like Draven."

Wendy shook her head. "I'm usually a coincidence kind of girl, but I think it's Draven."

"So wait a minute," Steve questioned. "You're telling me that the all-powerful wizard who has burned down villages, destroyed an academy, and killed people all in the name of the Ender Dragon, is actually a friendly castle wizard? How did people not know this?"

"It doesn't make sense, I agree," Wendy replied. "But it does look like him, doesn't it?"

Steve nodded, and they left the alleyway, going back to the inn the traditional way. As they made it back to the inn, they went back to their room.

"Now what should we do?" Wendy asked.

"I really want to see if Draven and Vradne are the same person," Steve told her.

"I agree. But how are we going to get to the tower if it's closed off? That seems a bit more difficult than the last time we infiltrated a tower."

"I don't even know. Let's see if Bartholomew's back," Steve suggested. They stood up and went to where Bartholomew's room was. There, they knocked on the door. Still no answer. They were about to return to their room when they saw him climbing up the stairs.

"It's you guys. Sorry, I was trying to get more information about old ruins around here," he stated.

"Find anything?" Steve asked.

"There's an old ruin south from here, but they say it's been cleaned out. I usually reply with 'challenge accepted,' but we have other things to worry about right now."

They explained about the tower and how they were going to get inside.

"I need to think about it, but are you sure that's a good idea? I know, me asking if that's a good idea is unusual, but still. Also, what was the wizard's name again?"

"Vradne," Steve replied.

"How do you spell that?"

Steve wondered why Bartholomew would care about that, but he told him. "V-R-A-D-N-E."

"It's an anagram," Bartholomew replied. "I've used those lots of times."

"An anagram?" Steve asked.

"It's when you rearrange the letters in a word to make something else. 'Vradne' has the same letters as 'Draven.'"

Steve looked as though his mind melted. "No way," he replied.

"I highly doubt it's a coincidence now. They're the same. The question is, how does he maintain a benevolent castle wizard and being a ruthless cult leader in one day?" Wendy asked.

"We'll find out," Bartholomew replied.

Steve wondered how they were going to get to the tower, and pondered what Draven's alter ego was like. Could Vradne be the good side of Draven, or were they two sides of the same coin?

Chapter Two

"So what should we do?" Wendy asked. "As much as I believe he's Draven, we need evidence before we go in that tower with our swords raised up high. If he's not, we're probably going to be arrested."

"And even if we're right, we could get arrested. It looks as though this guy is popular here," Steve replied.

"I say that we take a good look at him and make sure he's Draven. I mean, common sense points to that he is, but you never know. He could just be a person who has the same letters and a similar face," Bartholomew added. Then he uttered, "And has unsurpassed magic powers."

"Well, we're not getting a look at him unless we sneak in the tower. I didn't get a good look at the wizard's tower except for a glance, but it looks guarded," Steve replied.

"With my years of thieving, I know that anything can be infiltrated, no matter how guarded it is. But how should we handle it?" Bartholomew asked.

"We should go at night so we can escape easier and not attract too much attention," Wendy replied.

"True. And I have my ways of distracting guards, so we can get the two away while you guys slip in."

"That sounds like a plan," Steve replied, and they went back to their rooms to prepare for tonight. In their room, Steve prepared a few supplies while Wendy looked at herself in the mirror. She definitely wasn't the girl she was when she had left. She looked stronger, that was for sure.

"I feel bad sneaking into this castle. I mean, with my brot-, with Herobrine, it made sense. But I feel bad breaking into a castle where the king seems jolly. Plus, if we're wrong, what then?"

"Then we get out and look for Draven. If we don't hurt anyone in the process, we should be good," Wendy replied.

"True. It's just that I have a bad feeling about this. Almost as if Draven expects us. I want to end this, but at the same time, I don't feel strong enough to put an end to him."

"He is almost impossible to hurt," Wendy agreed. "But everyone has a weakness. I mean, he serves the Ender Dragon, so he should be weaker. And the Ender Dragon was defeated once before, so that should tell you something."

Steve nodded in agreement, but still… Draven had a core when he turned to bedrock, but it was only exposed when you damaged him when he was in a weaker state. From what he saw, Draven had to turn into diamond or dirt before he could upgrade to bedrock, so he had that one short chance to do damage. But if he messed it up, it could mean trouble. Bartholomew could save their skin again, but the entire kingdom would be after them.

They waited until nightfall and then they approached the castle, hiding behind buildings to make sure no one saw them. Once at the gates, they looked for a way over the fence without catching the attention of anyone. Guards stood in front of the gates, almost like statues. Their eyes kept shifting left and right, making sure that no one entered.

"What do you want to do?" Wendy asked the two of them. "Do you want to climb over the fence or do you want to distract the guards?"

"That fence looks high and it's pointed at the top, so it would be extremely difficult to cross without making too much of a ruckus," Steve replied.

"I have a few smoke bombs, but I feel like I would be alerting the entire castle if I use that."

"Wait, what about the rock trick?" Steve asked.

"What's that?" Wendy chimed in.

"When we entered Herobrine's castle, Bartholomew threw a rock past the guards to distract them. It was dumb enough to work," Steve told her.

Bartholomew had an embarrassed look on his face. "That was the old me. Besides, these guards look a little smarter than the ones at that gate."

"You never know until you try," Steve replied.

"Oh, fine. Let me find a rock."

Bartholomew ran away for a few minutes then returned holding a smooth stone. He ran towards the gate, sneaking along the fence, and then tossed the rock. His arm was strong, making the stone soar quite a distance. Immediately, the guards took off, and Bartholomew opened the gate. The three entered, Bartholomew closed the gate, and they snuck around the courtyard.

"I can't believe that stupid trick keeps working," Bartholomew whispered.

"I know, right? Don't they realize that you should go towards the source of the rock?" Wendy replied.

Past the courtyard, the tower stood. Two guards were at the door, and one of them yawned.

"I think our shift's over," the guard said.

"Well, do you want to alert the others to cover us?"

"Sure thing," the other guard said, and he walked towards the castle. They hid behind a cherry blossom tree as the guard passed them by.

"Just one left," Bartholomew whispered. He grabbed a stone and threw it towards the tower. It soared past the guard, but he didn't budge.

"What's his deal?" Steve asked.

They snuck closer to the tower, and that's when they heard the sound of snoring. After the other guard left, the lone one started snoring.

"He must have had a long day," Bartholomew said. He pulled out what appeared to be a hairpin and stood at the door, careful not to wake the sleeping soldier up. After fiddling with the lock a bit, the doors opened. They rushed inside and were greeted by a spiral staircase.

The room was lit with the faint glow of torches, and the whole place just looked foreboding. As they ascended the stairs, they were on the lookout for any tricks. They almost expected an army of mobs to attack, or for Draven to come out of nowhere and battle. But they eventually made it to the top without any worries, and that's when the huge, closed door greeted them. It was a wooden entrance that almost felt grand, like they were entering the lair of a powerful king. Bartholomew gently played with the knob, discovering that it was locked. However, a bit of lock picking fixed that. They opened the door, and prepared for what awaited them.

As it turned out, it appeared to be your ordinary wizard quarters. Potions were stacked alongside of a table, and there were three shelves of books on magic. A bed was at the corner, and as they approached it, they discovered Vradne asleep there, his hair covering the pillow. One look at his face confirmed it; he was Draven. However, he looked much different. His face had more color and he had a more innocent look on his face than expected. He seemed to be in a deep sleep, unaware that they stood in his room.

"This is probably the real Draven. His good side," Wendy declared. Steve just nodded.

"What are we going to do? We could kill him in his sleep, but even in my thieving days, that would be too cowardly."

"I agree. I don't want to kill him. I want to free him from the evil that is controlling him. Let's get back and make a plan."

As they exited his room, Draven started stirring in his bed. At first, they thought that he was going to wake up, but he ended up muttering in his sleep.

"No, daddy. Don't force me to become the Claw of the Ender. I just want to be a normal kid."

They left his tower, and they discussed what they saw.

"He's just an innocent boy who has succumbed to a great evil over the years," Bartholomew stated.

"Suddenly, I don't hate him as much. Rara's story was true. It's the people who raised him that made him that way, not himself. Therefore, we need to free him and make sure the evil that's controlling him is vanquished for good," Steve replied.

Outside of the tower, the guard was still sleeping. They made it out of there before the replacement guards could come, and they hugged the fence until they found a part where the spiked tips were more rounded, and there was no one around. They each took turns climbing the fence until they were over, and then they wondered what they would do next.

"I think that we need to prepare for battle," Steve said. "I don't know where we are going to battle him at, but we shall find out soon enough. Until then, let's get some rest."

They went back to the inn and they went back to their individual rooms, wondering what would happen next. Steve sat on his bed while looking at his sword.

"I hope I can defeat him. I don't even have any armor," he told Wendy.

"And armor would probably cost a lot," she replied.

"Not worth it. Anyway, Draven shattered my armor in one blow. It's only good to protect yourself once, and that makes it more expensive than it should be. I just need to dodge his attacks and I'll be fine."

"So, how are we going to fight him, anyway? His tower is a little closed off, and I don't want anyone getting hurt if we fight in the castle or at the courtyard. And how are we going to take him out without the wrath of every citizen upon us?"

Steve didn't know how that was going to work, but he was going to do it. While he was busy cleaning his sword, he stepped outside his room. It was late, but he didn't feel like sleeping yet. Wendy followed. Sure enough, they saw Elena standing outside of her room.

Steve and Wendy explained what they found, and Elena just sighed. "I know he's trapped, but I want you guys to show no mercy on him. Force him to give me back my father so my life can return to normal. I don't even care about living in a mansion anymore. I just want to see my dad again. I regret not spending more time with him when I had the chance. Once I became blinded with greed, I ignored him."

"It's alright," Steve replied. "I'm sure your father knows you love him. Besides that, I know he's still alive. So don't worry."

"I know. I just don't know what I'm going to do. I'm sick of being trapped in this inn. I'm tired of being in a town where I can't even walk around without feeling lost."

She almost began tearing up, then Wendy reached around to hug her. "Don't worry. We shall fix this."

"I hope you can," she told them as she headed back to her room. Meanwhile, they considered taking a walk outside, but they decided to instead get some sleep.

Wendy brewed some of the complimentary tea the inn provided with each room, made from herbs that could calm the nerves. Both of them sipped on the strong drink as they began talking about the future.

"So, once this is all over, do you want to-" Steve began, not knowing how to word it."

"Of course. Bring me home to your parents. But I need to get back to selling weapons once this is over, so if you don't mind working with me, then I'll gladly be your girlfriend."

"That doesn't sound like a bad trade," Steve happily replied.

Wendy smiled. "And since I own the business, I can take off whenever we want and have our own adventures."

They talked for a little while longer until the tea began hitting them. Eventually, they both passed out on their individual beds.

Chapter Three

When they woke up, they heard a commotion outside of the window. Steve looked outside while Wendy prepared some coffee. They saw a crowd walking towards a certain direction, and this piqued Steve's interest.

"What do you think's going on?" he asked.

Wendy handed him some coffee and they sipped on it. They needed to be as awake as possible if something were to happen. "I don't know. Why don't we find out?"

They finished their drinks and they rushed outside of the inn. There, Bartholomew stood, waiting on the two.

"What's going on?" Steve asked.

"Vradne is apparently going to speak in the town square," he replied.

Steve's eyes widened. All of these people were going to meet him? He knew how much the wizard was loved, but by almost everyone? They all looked eager to meet him, save for a few firm-looking parents who appeared to be angry over Vradne not letting their kids meet him yesterday.

"Let's see what he's up to," Wendy suggested, and they all took her lead. They followed the crowd, which soon became thick. They tried breaking through but were shoved back.

"Whoever decided to hold this meeting in the town square is an idiot," one stated. "Vradne is so popular, and this dinky little square can't hold his fans. Why not in the castle courtyard? Or better yet, outside of the town?"

People soon surrounded them. Steve felt claustrophobic while Wendy disliked the funk that came from the combined sweat and dirt from some of them. They felt as though they were about to meet someone famous. Steve knew that this whole crowd could turn into an angry mob if they engaged Draven. They also even managed to become separated from Bartholomew.

The crowd finally stopped moving. Steve hopped in the air because the people in front of him were taller than he was. He could see the square in front of them, but there was literally no more room for them to move. Everyone was packed in there as tight as possible. How would Draven even get through the crowd to enter?

There was a small clock tower near the square and many checked the tower's clock with impatience. "He said he was supposed to be here five minutes ago. What's taking him so long?"

This one loner questioning the delay soon turned into the entire crowd chattering at one another. People thought that he died, or that he abandoned them. Steve and Wendy waited while their stomachs began churning. Someone not showing up was just a minor annoyance most of the time, but with every waking second, they wondered what Draven had planned.

The chattering soon turned to gasps. Steve hopped to see what was going on. Now Draven stood in the center of the stage, with Steve assuming that he teleported.

"Here, hop on my shoulders," Wendy told Steve. Steve did just that, and Wendy piggybacked him so that he could see.

Now that he had a more detailed look of Draven's face, he noticed just how meek he looked. His cold eyes looked warm, his skin was not pale but more of a creamy hue, and his hair was combed and looked clean. He smiled at the crowd as they cheered, and when he started talking, his voice sounded calm and barely resembled the voice he used when he was about to murder them.

"Sorry for ignoring you guys for so long and sorry for the delay in showing up," Draven declared, giving the crowd a loving smile. They went wild, even those who were giving Draven flack for not being there for the meet and greet yesterday.

Draven cleared his throat, raising his arms in a grand manner. "This kingdom has many great things in store for it. Did I say kingdom? I meant the entire world."

A few of the audience members chatted amongst themselves, wondering what he meant.

"Are you going to become king of the world? That would be awesome!" a child shouted from the crowd. This caused the audience to go wild with applause.

Draven let out a hearty laugh, but then he replied with "Now, now. Simmer down you all. I'm not going to become king of the world…but I do have a friend who is."

They all started talking once again. Some were skeptical, yet others thought that a friend of Vradne must be a good thing. When the talking stopped, Draven began speaking again.

"For too long, we've been under the rule of too many leaders. Kings, councilmen, guards, the wealthy. It's enough to make anyone's head spin. This is why I have great news regarding that. My friend will rule this world and no one else. There will be no more poverty, inequality, or corrupt systems. This person treats everyone equally."

The crowd began conversing. "This sounds too good to be true!" one said. "I agree. I almost feel like Vradne's pulling our legs. He's been known for being a prankster!"

Draven laughed. "I swear to you that it's not a prank. Has anyone heard about the legend of the Ender Dragon?"

"I have!" a kid declared. "Mommy reads it to me every night before I go to bed."

Draven smiled. "Very good. But it's not just a fairy tale. What if I were to tell you that it's a true story, and that the Ender Dragon is returning to rule us all?"

"Is the Ender Dragon the one you're talking about? But he's evil!" the kid replied. The crowd stared at Draven with blank looks, not knowing if he was being serious or had lost his marbles.

"Time has not been kind to the Ender Dragon's reign. Rulers have published lies about him, claiming that he was an evil force. In truth, he brought balance to this world, but those who wanted power defeated him. I've been working to bring him back and return true equality to this world!"

So far, Draven didn't even look at Steve, who was unsure if Draven knew he was in the crowd. With him, it could go either way. However, Wendy seemed a bit strained over holding Steve up for so long, so he hopped off her.

"Does he really believe that the Ender Dragon is just?" Steve asked. "I mean, come on. With all of the actions that have happened because of him, I hardly believe that."

"Draven is full of himself," Wendy replied. "But part of me thinks that he really believes, or was conditioned to believe, that the Ender Dragon is a force for good."

The crowd still seemed invested as they heard Draven continue.

"In fact, he's resurrected already. But he's at The End, recovering. At this rate, however, it will take a millennium for him to get back to full strength. But this is where you guys come in. You see, the Ender Dragon becomes stronger when it consumes souls. This crowd has enough souls to get him to full strength and maybe more."

"Wait, what are you saying!" one shouted. The crowd began murmuring. They didn't want to believe that Vradne was up to something, but it was looking grimmer by the minute. Steve hopped and noticed the gradual change in Draven's appearance. Now he resembled his evil self, and Steve wanted to get through the crowd to defeat him.

"Is he going to take everyone's souls? Wendy asked. "That sounds insane even for him. Was this his motivation all this time? No wonder he wanted us out of the picture."

Behind them, they could hear the sound of someone squeezing through the crowd. They turned around to see that it was Bartholomew. "Even for a stealthy person like me, getting through the crowd was almost impossible. But I've heard everything, and we must put a stop to this."

"But how are we going to get through the crowd?" Steve asked.

"Use your head! Or rather, their heads," Bartholomew replied, smirking.

"Do you mean-"

Before Steve could finish, Bartholomew hopped on his shoulders and propelled himself above the crowd, his feet stepping on the crowd's heads in a light manner, but enough for them to become agitated. Steve hopped on Wendy's shoulders and he began moving across the crowd, becoming imbalanced as they tried to shake him off. Wendy hopped on another person and began moving. Soon they landed at the center platform where Draven spoke.

"Don't worry, the soul won't be lost forever, and-"

They looked at him and brandished their weapons.

"And here we have a few people who want to put a stop to my plans. What, don't you want humanity to become equal?" as he spoke, his voice lowered to sound like the Draven that they knew.

Steve shook his head. "I'd love for everyone to live equally, but it doesn't count when the only reason that they are is because they're being forced to by an all-powerful dragon!"

Draven made a *tsk tsk* as he eyed them. "The method of how they are equal doesn't matter. The fact of the matter is, they are going to be treated normally, regardless of income, gender, or any physical difference."

"And you're going to sacrifice this entire crowd to do so," Wendy stated.

Draven grinned. "A means to an end. You have to sacrifice something for the greater good, after all."

A few of the crowd members tried climbing on stage, but a barrier caused them to fall back. Some tried leaving the square, but the same force surrounded all sides. Draven trapped everyone. They were his own sheep about to become slaughtered, but not before they were spectators to the fight that was about to unfold.

"No one is going to be sacrificed. Not even you, Draven! We know your story. You're just a poor child who is trapped by the forces of the Ender Dragon. We are going to free you, defeat the evil, and then defeat the Ender Dragon!" Steve spoke, while Draven laughed.

"You make good speeches for a man who has such short-term memory. Have you forgotten how many times you've lost against me? How many times you've had to run away? What makes this fight any different? You don't have any new equipment and I doubt you can improve yourself that much over the course of only a few days," Draven retorted.

"And I thought I was cocky when I was a thief," Bartholomew declared.

Draven eyed Bartholomew. "You were the one who saved their behinds last time. Hmm, for some reason, I get a strange vibe from you, the same feeling I experienced with those two. Could you be…?"

"What are you blabbing on about?" Bartholomew asked.

Draven began laughing, and this agitated Bartholomew. "Just tell me!"

Draven stopped. "Oh, has fate been too kind. The Ender Dragon does work in great and mysterious ways. Let me explain. I've been hunting the boy and girl because they are the descendants of two of the three heroes who slayed the Ender Dragon all of these years ago. But that still leaves one. I feel it in my gut. You're the third descendent. This is glorious! I can kill all three of you right here, and no one can stop the Ender Dragon!"

Bartholomew smirked. "Hero? I grew up with a family of thieves. I no longer am one myself, but I still work for no one but me. And you're telling me that I have some great destiny to slay an Ender Dragon? Forget it. But I'll bite. Let's go!"

Draven still kept his smile while Steve and Wendy stood there in awe. Bartholomew was the third descendent? Steve almost killed him when they first clashed, which seemed like ages ago. If he had died, then what?

"Okay," Draven declared. "Enough fighting! It's time to end you three and then the Ender Dragon shall return! Come at me and meet your deaths!"

Chapter Four

Steve took out his sword, Wendy took out a blade she carried, and Bartholomew unsheathed two daggers. Draven began shooting projectiles at them, which they managed to dodge. Some soared past them and hit the barrier, causing them to dissipate. Steve rushed towards Draven, and Steve brought out his sword. Immediately, Draven transformed to diamond, and Steve's sword hit his arm. Steve thought about dirt, and then Draven's entire body turned to that.

Okay, I only have one chance to do this! Steve thought. He began slashing at Draven's chest, the dirt falling in clumps. This revealed a hollow inside, and suspended in the center was a glowing ball of white light. The same white light that Steve encountered. Draven changed himself to bedrock and was about to block Steve's blow, but then Steve jabbed the sword inside, going right through the white ball.

As soon as the blade sunk inside, everything went white for Steve. He walked across a void made of nothing but dead white light. At first, he thought that he'd be walking there forever, but then he saw someone else. It was a boy about his age. One glance revealed that the boy was a child Draven.

Draven looked at Steve and widened his eyes. "Please, mister. Could you get me out of this place? It feels like I've been walking here for an eternity. Sometimes I feel like I've found the way out, but as soon as I poke my head through it, I return to this void."

"I don't know how to get here myself," Steve replied. This caused Draven's eyes to well up, and Steve rushed to comfort him. Draven soon cried, in hysterics.

"My dad told me that I have to fulfill the prophecy. I must create a group of devoted Ender Dragon followers and give the Ender Dragon the strength it needs when it does return. But I don't want to do that! I want to be an ordinary boy. I wanted to be a wizard who helps people, not one who hurts. But my dad cast a spell on me to bring out my dark side."

"Dark side?" Steve asked.

"Everyone has one. Some are more powerful than others. My dark side turned out to be powerful. But who could blame me? They abused me and forced me into a life I didn't want. At first, the dark side only came out every now and then and I was only sent here briefly. But now, I've been sent here for what seems like forever. It could be days, months, or even years. I just want to get out!"

Steve didn't feel like telling him the truth that Draven had been in there for decades upon decades. Instead, he let Draven continue to rant.

"I don't want the Ender Dragon to be released. I just want to be a normal boy. The world is flawed, but the Ender Dragon isn't going to fix that."

Steve nodded. "Indeed it isn't."

Draven put his hands on his heads and began trembling in anxiety. "How do I get out of here?"

All of a sudden, the entire void began trembling. Steve felt as though it was trying to pull him out. He flew back, and while he did, he shouted towards Draven.

"You can break free. Believe in yourself, and you should be able to defeat the evil within!"

Steve flew backwards, and when he looked ahead, he saw that he was back at the platform that Draven stood on. Wendy and Bartholomew looked at him, glad to see that he was okay, and Steve stood up. While he did, Draven repaired his body until he was back to normal. Then he looked at him while laughing.

"You've failed! Now there's nothing that you can do to defeat me!"

The crowd surrounding them was in even more hysterics. Some attempted to break through the barrier yet again, but the barrier kicked them back once again.

"Poor little people. No one can save them now. You had a chance to free them, but now you've lost!"

Draven charged at them, his bedrock fists raised. Steve dodged and Wendy ducked. Bartholomew threw a smoke bomb, but it only annoyed Draven, and once the smoke cleared, he tried attacking again. Soon he cornered Steve and attacked. Steve rolled under his legs and Draven turned around to strike again. Steve protected his sword and struck Draven when he could. Despite the sword not being powerful enough to change Draven's bedrock body back to normal, he kept trying. What else could he do?

The others knew that they had to be the sitting ducks in this battle, or rather, the dodging ducks. Draven went after Wendy a few times, but Wendy managed to avoid his attacks. But not for long. Draven cornered Wendy and pressed his legs together so she couldn't escape, and then he raised his arms to swing. While Bartholomew was busy preparing another smoke bomb, Steve ran to save Wendy. He hopped over Draven's back and held his sword up, Draven's punch rammed Steve's sword. All of a sudden, Steve's blade shattered into many pieces. In the chaos, Wendy managed to escape, and now it was Draven against Steve.

"I knew that the girl could be used to your advantage," Draven gloated. And now you're cornered. I shall punch the lights out of you and then make you watch as the return of the Ender Dragon happens. It's going to be glorious!"

Draven raised his fists in order to attack Steve, and before he could swing, he stopped.

No! I'm not going to let you!

"Huh?" Draven shouted. Steve was also confused. The voice sounded disembodied, but at the same time, seemed like it was right next to Steve.

Steve was right! All I needed to do was to believe in myself and I could break free from your grip! For too long, I was not confident enough to think I could escape. But Steve, in only a few minutes, gave me enough strength for me to do it!

"Shut up, you little brat! You can't get out of here, and you know it. I've imprisoned you inside me!"

That may be true, but I realize that I can stop some of your attacks. Watch this!

All of a sudden, Draven's bedrock body vanished, leaving behind his fleshy form. Draven attempted to transform back, but failed. He tried casting spells on the three, but nothing happened.

"What's going on? How could this happen?" he cried.

The disembodied voice was silent. Steve, Wendy, and Bartholomew ganged up on him, with the latter two raising their weapons.

Draven should have been begging for his life, but instead he was laughing. At first, it was a light chuckle, but soon he made a hearty belly laugh.

"What's so funny?" Wendy asked. "We have you cornered. You can't use magic!"

Draven grinned. "Most magic, anyway. The Ender Dragon granted me a spell that cannot be suppressed. It was the spell that will trigger the ritual. I wanted to defeat you all before doing it, but I guess I have no choice."

Draven raised his arms in the air, and they ran towards him. However, they were only a few inches away before something knocked them back. They fell to the ground flat on their backs, and they could see the sky darkening. At first, a few black clouds covered the area, but then so many blanketed around that it looked like a night sky without the stars. The audience noticed this as well, and they began looking up. Lightning flew from the clouds, striking no one. It almost felt like it was there just for show.

"Watch and behold. You three will be safe because you're sitting on this platform. But the rest? They're going to be soul food!"

All of a sudden, a swirling black vortex appeared in the sky, looking powerful enough to absorb everyone. But it didn't do that. Instead, the audience, all of them staring at it, dropped to the floor. Because of its density, the bodies piled up. When they fell down, a wisp of white light flew from the beings, and the void sucked them all up until they were gone.

"And now everyone's soul is taken. Too bad. Their bodies are now empty husks, waiting for their soul to return. They're trapped in limbo, and I can feel the Ender Dragon as it devours the souls."

Steve yelled and ran to Draven, but the barrier knocked him back. While that happened, Draven began laughing.

"Oh, it's just beginning. Now you'll see the Ender Dragon return. You've missed your brother, so I'll allow you to see him. Hope you say hi."

Steve shouted at Draven, but he knew it was no use. In the end, the three just looked upwards as something flew out of the portal. It was the Ender Dragon.

"That thing looks bigger than before," Wendy stated.

Maybe he couldn't remember the Ender Dragon's exact details, but Steve realized that she was right. The Ender Dragon was around twice the size as it was when the revival happened. Its wingspan covered the entire town square, and the wings looked like translucent obsidian. Its teeth looked sharp enough to break a mountain apart. The tail looked as though as diamond.

The Ender Dragon let out a roar, almost like it was waking up from a long nap. Draven looked at the Ender Dragon, smiling.

"Did I do well? I told you that I would help to bring you back, and I was right. Change this world for the better! I'll deal with these three."

The Ender Dragon roared again, and began flapping its wings. While it passed over the town, it opened its mouth, black flames spilling from it. They landed all over the village, and suddenly the kingdom was engulfed in them save for the part still protected by the barrier.

"Herobrine!" Steve shouted, trying to jump out of the barrier. But he could not. Instead, he looked at Draven. "Are you insane? You've brought upon the end of the world as we know it."

Draven nodded. "Precisely. Soon, the Ender Dragon will make the world bow to its every will. Kings and other leaders will be equal to the lowliest peasant. No matter how hard they struggle, they will not defeat him. Because I will kill you three right now and end the bloodline of the heroes for good."

"No, you're wrong!" Steve declared. "You're not going to defeat us. We've gone on for too long, experienced too much, just to lose from you. Everyone you and the Ender Dragon have taken from us: my brother, Rara, this entire town, all will be saved. And so will you, Draven."

"We're not going to sit by while the Ender Dragon takes over," Wendy added.

"We're going to kick both your butts," Bartholomew chimed in.

Draven let out a chuckle. "Enough with your cheesy speeches. You know that you're not going to end, so why don't we end this?"

He shot a projectile out, a fireball that passed over their heads. Once again, it hit the barrier and vanished.

"Look at that, I'm finally getting the brat to shut up. You'll be next," Draven claimed.

Please, you have to stop him. I'm losing control. I'm still stopping him from changing his body, but he still has his magic powers. You need to defeat him quickly, or you're not going to win, the voice groaned from nowhere.

"Try it. The boy has no weapons, the girl doesn't have much combat experience, and the man is quick, but I shall swat him like a fly," Draven said.

"I'd like to see you try," Bartholomew replied, staring Draven down.

Draven smiled. "Oh, indeed I will."

They looked at the burning kingdom surrounding them. Everything was at stake here, and if they lost, there wouldn't be any hope left for this world. They looked at one another and made a nod, and then they rushed towards Draven.

Chapter Five

Draven shot out a burst of wind, and the three fell to the ground. They picked up their weapons and looked at the mad cultist, who just smiled as he fired another blast of wind. Steve pressed his feet against the ground, resisting Draven's attack. Bartholomew ran against the wind and threw a smoke bomb at Draven. It exploded under his feet. Bartholomew rushed in the cloud of smoke, but Draven teleported out of it, firing three fireballs into the thick fog.

Bartholomew jumped out before they could hit him, and he looked at Draven, who smiled. "You three have a long way to go before you can defeat me," he told them. Firing a bolt of lightning at Steve, he laughed as Steve jumped out of the way.

I'm nothing without my sword, Steve thought to himself. If he could get close, he could land a few punches, but Steve was not an expert with hand-to-hand combat. Besides that, did he want to get that close to a man who could vaporize him in one blow?

Steve got close to Draven, but not close enough to where he could try anything that Steve couldn't dodge. All of a sudden, Draven ran towards him, his fists raised. It looked like he had read his mind. He swung his fist at him, and Steve jumped out of the way. Steve countered by giving him an uppercut on the chin. He didn't even realize how powerful the blow was until it knocked Draven back. Draven rubbed the sore spot on his chin, and then electricity began surging through his fists.

"Oh, it's on now," he declared. Wendy and Bartholomew jumped towards Draven, but Draven punched both of them in the gut. They flew back, electricity flowing through their bodies for a brief second. They did not move after that.

"You monster!" Steve shouted, and he ran towards Draven. Draven swung his fists, but Steve managed to block. Steve countered by kicking him in the shin, causing Draven to squeal in pain. Their heads clashed together, and both flew back.

"I'm just holding back," Draven declared. I know you're no match for me when it comes to unarmed combat, so I'm going easy on you. Now it's time to show you what I can do."

The electricity began flowing faster through his knuckles, and Draven ran to Steve. Steve dodged three of his punches, but the fourth clocked him in the stomach. Steve felt the shock and it seemed like he would explode at any second. But Steve managed to stand his ground. Draven punched him in the arms, and his limbs felt nonexistent when that happened. Then, with one final blow, Steve received a shocking punch to the chin. His entire brain felt haywire for a few seconds, and Steve flew back, falling to the ground. He tried to get up, but the pain was too much. Draven stood in the center of the triangle of wounded warriors, laughing at his victory.

"Now, what should I do with you three? I could kill you all, but I also want you to suffer greatly. How about if I spare your lives by sending you to where Rara's staying right now? An eternity of suffering, but at least you'll be in good company."

A mass of dark matter grew in each hand of Draven. His hands pointed at Wendy and Bartholomew. "Now then, I think I'm going to take them out first."

The orbs fired from his hands, and Steve shouted in anger.

"Now!" Wendy shouted. Before the orbs hit the bodies, Bartholomew and Wendy stood up and ran past them, the orbs hitting the barrier. Draven stood there in shock, and began shooting projectiles at the two. However, his spell required an excessive amount of power, and he hadn't recharged. He attempted teleporting away, but he could not.

Wendy kicked Draven in the stomach while Bartholomew took out his hidden dagger, stabbing him in the right leg. He pulled it out and stabbed his left one. Draven fell to the ground, and the two pinned his arms down using their feet.

"I can't believe we're working together," Wendy exclaimed.

"You're telling me," Bartholomew replied. Both stared down Draven.

"How… did you…" Steve croaked.

"We're tougher than that. As we were attacking him, both of us had the plan to pretend to be more injured than we were. His punch is tough, but it's not enough to knock us out for good," Wendy exclaimed.

However, Steve received multiple punches, and he could barely move.

"Return their souls," Wendy told Draven.

Draven let out a wheezing laugh. "It's too late. They are a part of the Ender Dragon now. I may have lost the battle, but I've taken the right steps to win the war. It's too late. In a matter of weeks, this world will be ruined by the Ender Dragon, and he shall reign supreme from The End. It shall be glorious."

Wendy punched him in the face, and Draven kept laughing. "You couldn't even free the boy. How do you expect to-"

No, you're wrong. I've figured out how to destroy you. You're going down with me, the voice declared.

"What's that?" Draven shouted, but before anyone could answer, Draven's mouth opened. A white wisp, looking similar to the souls that came from the audience, spilled out of him. This soul, however, seemed brighter than most.

Perhaps one day my soul will be reborn, and I can live the life I wanted. Until then, its farewell, the soul spoke. It then vanished.

Draven began laughing harder than ever. "Without the soul of the boy, I can't control this body for long. However, my final words are this. I may return from the darkness from whence I came, but as I disappear, I will be remembering how I fulfilled the wishes of the cult. Now it's time to leave this world and hopefully be one with the Ender Dragon!"

Draven's mouth spread open, and a black gas, almost as thick as smoke, expelled from him. It floated in the air for a few seconds and then began to dissipate. Wendy and Bartholomew looked at Draven's body to discover that there was no life left in it. Like the others, he was just an empty husk.

Bartholomew walked towards the edge of the platform to discover that the barrier was gone. Meanwhile, Wendy approached Steve, who appeared to be unconscious. She picked him up and they stepped off the platform. The fires disappeared as almost as quickly as they spread, and the entire town, save for the square, was in a giant pile of ash. They had to make their way around bodies, and Wendy noticed one in particular that made her gasp.

It was Elena. She made it to the square, but her soul had been taken like everyone else's. Her body an empty husk, Wendy wondered if Elena and the rest of them could still be saved. If they defeated the Ender Dragon, would they be able to return everyone's souls back to normal? Even the good side of Draven?

They walked amongst the ash, and all that time, Wendy never let go of Steve.

Steve and Herobrine were always the brothers who raced each other whenever they had the chance. As such, they took off in a heated run whenever they felt like it, and this led to some intense competition. They decided to visit the local forest, and soon they ended up running across the forest. It was all going well at first. Steve and Herobrine were close, with Steve leading the way by a few feet. Then, Herobrine tripped over a tree root. He spilled on the ground, his arms and knees scraped. Herobrine cried about it for a while, even more so when they went home and Steve wiped the blood from his wounds with a wet cloth. Then he practically screamed when his parents poured the alcohol over his wounds.

But it wasn't just the pain. At night, he asked Steve if he did something wrong. He felt almost guilty over a simple trip.

"I feel as though I made a huge mistake. I should have been watching where I was going. And now my arms and legs are going to look funny for at least a month."

Steve smiled and tried comforting him the best he could. "Everyone falls and hurts themselves every once in a while. You just have to get up, try not to make the same mistakes again, and reach for your goal." Steve was regurgitating something his teacher taught him, but it made Herobrine feel more comfortable. And sure enough, a couple of weeks later, they raced again in the woods, and Herobrine won.

Steve opened his eyes, and by then, it was nightfall. A fire flickered in front of him, and Wendy and Bartholomew were busy cooking a sheep they found in the field. When Steve glanced around, he noticed how the land looked like it was slowly dying. The vegetation looked burnt, and the animals moved around in a frantic mess.

"What happened?" Steve asked.

"You were out for about ten hours," Wendy replied.

"My body feels awful. What happened with Draven?"

Wendy and Bartholomew explained how they weren't able to save the good side of Draven. Steve sighed, feeling like a failure. Draven defeated him and Wendy and Bartholomew barely won. The town they were in had their souls taken while the Ender Dragon kept burning everything down. According to Wendy, they stopped by a few villages, but they were all in ruins.

"The Ender Dragon has destroyed people's homes. Villagers are left to wander around, and I wonder what the Ender Dragon is going to do next," Wendy exclaimed.

"I wish we knew more about it," Bartholomew added.

Steve almost forgot how they were looking for more information about the Ender Dragon before being pulled into the cult stuff. Now that the Claw of the Ender was no more, Steve wondered if they could find anything. However, if everything was in ashes, then he doubted he could find much.

"What should we do?" he asked.

"I don't know. All that I know is that we're the three who are destined to slay the Ender Dragon," Wendy replied.

"I still can't believe it myself. Me? A hero? I didn't think that was possible," Bartholomew replied. He had a laugh at this, but Steve couldn't find anything funny.

I feel like I could have defeated Draven before he could restore the Ender Dragon back to his full power. And now the world is in ruins and we have no idea of where to go, he thought. He wanted to just quit now, feeling as though he wasn't a hero.

However, he began thinking about the dream he had about Herobrine and how Herobrine blamed himself for his fall. Steve could still remember that day, and it was almost as though Herobrine sent him a sign for him to keep going. Steve fell twice. Once when he tried to save Herobrine, and another when he tried saving Draven. But he could still move, and there was still an opportunity to save everyone. The Ender Dragon could still be defeated, and everyone who was affected by all of this could return. Steve needed to get up from his fall and not make the same mistake ever again.

The next morning, everything still seemed dark outside. It felt as though the world was stuck in twilight forever, and as they continued, Steve spoke to Wendy and Bartholomew.

"Let's make this right. We shall find out how to reach the Ender Dragon, and when we do, we shall defeat it and save everyone. No failing."

Wendy and Bartholomew nodded, and Wendy took Steve's hand. Together, they walked across the ruined world, looking for anything that would help them out. Despite the grim outlook, Steve hoped that they would find something that could defeat the Ender Dragon for good.

CPSIA information can be obtained at www.ICGtesting.com
Printed in the USA
LVOW08s1847140115

422824LV00010B/279/P